WESTERHAM WITCHES AND AN AUSSIE MISADVENTURE

PARANORMAL INVESTIGATION BUREAU

BOOK XX

DIONNE LISTER

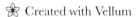

CHAPTER 1

I stepped out of the bright sunshine and into coffee-scented heaven. Holding Will's hand, I strode up to the counter of Surfer's Brew, grinning.

It was so good to be back.

"Oh my God, Lily, is that really you?!" Ah, how I'd missed Australian accents. Something I never thought I'd say. Frances hurried from behind the counter and pounced on me. Her hug was unexpected but nice. When I'd lived in Cronulla, I'd been a regular customer, but we hadn't been best friends. Even so, we sometimes ran into each other out and about and hung out at the pub, and to be fair, I'd been gone for almost two years. It was nice that she'd obviously missed me.

I stepped back. "Yep. We flew in from London last night." I shook my head. "Look at you. You haven't changed a bit." She was still slim and gorgeous with silky blonde hair, which was up in her usual ponytail. At least some things never changed. I inhaled the sweet coffee-bean fragrance. "I've missed you and this place. You guys make some of the best coffee ever."

Will smirked. "Don't let anyone from Costa hear you say that. Traitor."

Frances looked at Will, her appreciative gaze travelling from his face to his feet and back. She turned to me. "So, who's this hottie with the sexy accent?"

I chuckled. She wasn't going for subtle this morning. I held up my hand and wiggled my ring finger. "My fiancé. But don't tell him he's hot because I'll never hear the end of it. He's going to have even more tickets on himself now."

Beren laughed from behind us. "It's too late, Lily. But it's not too late for you to back away slowly and run. You still have ten days to come to your senses."

Liv smacked his arm. "Don't even joke about it. You might've cursed the wedding now."

Will grabbed my hand and looked at Liv. "Nothing is stopping us from getting married before we leave Australia, Liv. There's nothing I wouldn't do to make it happen." His blue-grey eyes locked on mine, and yes, I swooned. I was only human.

Frances grinned. "You two make a gorgeous couple. So, you're tying the knot in ten days. Where are you having the wedding?"

"One of Mum's old friends has a place at Mosman, overlooking the harbour. The grounds are gorgeous. We were lucky she was okay with it because it's fairly last minute." Frances peered at my belly. I laughed. "Ha, no way. I'm not pregnant. Work was just frantic before we left, and the trip was a spur-of-the-moment thing." I was still recovering from the surprise they'd unleashed on the plane when I was supposedly investigating a bomb threat. After they'd informed me we were coming to Australia, we'd all taken our seats, and here we were.

She nodded slowly. "So, have you got the catering organised? I might know someone." She winked.

I looked at Will, and he gave a subtle nod. I turned back to Frances. "As a matter of fact, no. We were all going to pitch in and do it, but if you're offering your services…."

"Since you left, I bought the café, and I've started a weekend catering business. I work here Monday to Friday, and my partner, Cory, works here with a couple of my staff on the weekends. I happen to have no bookings for the next two weeks, so I'm available."

"Ooh, partner as in business or partner as in boyfriend?" Life moved on, even when you weren't around to see it, and I was kind of sad that I'd missed so much. I was catching up with my two Sydney besties, Simone and Michelle, at the local pub, Northies, tonight for dinner. They'd both said yes to coming to the wedding, which was great since I hadn't given them much notice.

She cocked her head to the side and gave me a sweet smile. "Both."

"You can bring him too. I mean, I'll pay for the food of course, but you can both come as guests. My mum's hired someone to clean up afterwards, so you won't have to worry about that." Okay, so we were going to use magic to clean up, but I couldn't tell Frances that.

"Really? That would be awesome. Thank you! And you've picked a wonderful spot. I've always loved Sydney Harbour. My grandfather used to take me sailing around there when I was young. Watching the sunset from his yacht and then the city lights come alive one by one is one of my favourite memories. What a gorgeous place to get married."

One of her staff, a young guy with surfie-blond hair in waves to his shoulders, called out while frothing some milk. "Frances, I hate to break up the reunion, but…."

A line had formed, and we hadn't even ordered our coffees yet either. She bit her bottom lip. "Oops, gotta get back to it. Leave me your email address, and I'll send you our menu and prices this arvo. Just let me know what you want and how many people."

"Will do."

She grabbed my hand and gave it a squeeze. "It's so good to have you back in Sydney, Lily."

I grinned. "It's good to be back." I hadn't let myself think of home much in England because it made me sad—it was hard to be torn between two places you loved. But now we were here, I was totally going to make the most of it, and that would start with a cup of my favourite coffee, and if everything went to plan, my trip would end after I married the most amazing man in the universe. I didn't think I'd ever been happier. This was going to be the best holiday ever.

CHAPTER 2

Northies was as I remembered—loud music, crowded, and good food. I ate the last bite of my chicken parmigiana, grateful that I was wearing a loose-fitting dress. "Mmm, their parmis are to die for. I'm never disappointed."

Will patted his stomach. "I enjoyed it. They certainly give good portion sizes."

Simone, who sat between me and her partner, Rob, grabbed my hand, and I turned to her. "I'm just happy to have you back. You left so suddenly." Her sad blue eyes gave me all the guilts.

"I know. I'm sorry, but how could I not go? James was missing. There's no way I was going to wait and see if they found him." I'd told her that he was kidnapped and then found. I'd downplayed what had happened, not telling her about my time in jail or almost getting killed by the psycho who'd kidnapped him. And, of course, I'd said nothing about us being witches.

"Yeah, I know, but still. We missed you. Besides, you didn't come straight back when you found him." She raised a brow, then looked across the table at our blonde friend Michelle.

Michelle gave me a "she's right" look, but then she broke out a smile. "Simone's right, but at least you had the decency to come back here to get married. I would've been on the first plane over there with marzipan if I'd heard we'd missed your wedding."

I chuckled. My friends had known I hated marzipan since that time I threw up at Michelle's sixteenth birthday. She'd given me a chocolate—little did I know what was inside. Ever since then, it had been a running joke that if anyone wanted to clear a room, just make me eat marzipan. "Yes, well, I wasn't going to let you ladies miss this."

"Have you got it all organised?" Simone asked.

"Pretty much. Frances has agreed to do the food, and we've got that place I told you about at Mosman. Mum's helping me source a dress this week, and we've got the cake and photos organised. I can't believe we pulled it together so quickly." Being a witch had its perks. Not that I could tell them that the cake could be magicked together in a matter of minutes, as could my dress. Mum used to sew the old-fashioned, non-witch way, so she knew what she was doing. We were going to buy some fabric tomorrow and look through some photos of what I wanted. Like the cake, the dress would only take a few minutes. It was kind of complicated to imagine the spell, but Mum insisted it was easy for her, and who was I to argue?

"I couldn't believe it when you told us you found your mum." Michelle shook her head. "It's good that she got her memory back." I'd told the girls that Mum had amnesia and had finally remembered who she was and that she'd found us via Angelica. It sounded crazy, but the truth was even more unbelievable, so we'd gone with the daytime-soapie version. "And Frances is awesome." Michelle smiled. "She catered my dad's fiftieth when she started. We were her first freelance catering job. The food was amazing."

Not that I'd been concerned, but that eased some of my nerves. Even though we were witches and had this thing almost fully organised, things could still go wrong, and I hadn't even done a taste testing with her and wasn't going to that I knew of. The thing I was most worried about was the weather because that was one thing even Angelica couldn't control. The forecast said showers, which wasn't ideal, but showers could mean light rain first thing in the morning and sunny for the rest of the day, or it might be wrong, and it could storm or be sunny the whole day. Sometimes the weather bureau stuffed it up even the day before, so I wasn't going to count my chickens until the morning of.

After dinner, we sat around and had a couple of drinks. Liv, Beren, Imani, Sarah, and Lavender had come with us to experience an Aussie pub. James and Millicent had stayed in with the baby, and Mum, Angelica, and Phillip had gone out to one of the nicer restaurants on the beach called Summer Salt.

At midnight, they called last drinks, and I said bye to the girls. Crazily, I agreed to an early morning walk on the beach. I hadn't seen them for so long, so I wasn't going to miss any opportunity to catch up. I hugged my friends. "See you ladies at six tomorrow morning."

"And this is how I know you still love us." Simone chuckled. My friends knew I had an aversion to rising early. They both jogged at five thirty every day. They'd convinced me once, and that had been the only time. My body didn't appreciate me waking it up and forcing it to exercise before it was good and ready.

My English posse and I crossed the road to Rydges hotel, which had beach views. My flat was rented out, so Will and I had to go full tourist too. Not that I minded. The facilities were more than comfortable, and it felt like a true holiday. "So, how did you enjoy your first day in Oz?"

Everyone grinned, and Liv answered, "I'm surprised you didn't come straight back after you saved James. This place is gorgeous—the beach, the sun, the relaxed vibe." She looked at Beren. "Maybe we should all move here."

He laughed as we got into the elevator. "I could be persuaded."

Sarah looked at Will. "Mum and Dad would never forgive us." She turned her eyes my way. "You wouldn't move back, would you?"

"Never say never, but I'm enjoying England, and wherever my friends and Will are, that's where I want to be."

Both Will's eyebrows jumped up. "Why did you mention me last? Am I second best now you know you've got me?"

I knew he was kidding. "Well, third best if you count Abby, Ted, and the squirrels. Actually, that's why I could never move back here for good—I couldn't bear to leave my squirrel army."

Lavender snorted, and Imani said, "That's our Lily. At least we know where we stand."

Will gave me a mock devastated look and put his hands over his heart. "Oh, how you wound me."

"Fine. You're my number one. Is that better?"

He smiled. "Much."

We said goodnight to everyone and retired to our room. I dreaded setting the alarm so early, especially since I was still a bit jet-lagged and wasn't tired right now. Hopefully, I'd fall asleep by one and at least get four hours sleep.

Hope was for suckers.

My alarm went off after I'd managed to have about an hour's sleep. Yay me. Not. I magicked on black knee-length tights and a red razorback top. Sneakers tied, I tiptoed out of the room, leaving my gorgeous man asleep.

The morning sun sat just over the horizon, but joggers and surfers were already out and about in the end-of-spring warmth. Seagulls bobbed beyond the line of surfers awaiting a wave, and the air misted with fine salty spray. I breathed it in. *Ah, it was good to be back.* Maybe getting up early wasn't so bad when this was my reward.

Michelle and Simone, both dressed in workout gear, stood at the Cronulla memorial for the Bali bombing victims. A large, rounded, pinkish-grey stone, it represented a place locals could remember the seven Sutherland Shire women that never came home. Two hundred and two people lost their lives in that bombing, which was two hundred and two too many. I hadn't known any of them, but I took a moment to acknowledge the lives that were cut short.

"Lily!" Simone pulled me in for a hug, and Michelle joined us. We all squeezed tightly.

My "It's good to be back" was muffled by Simone's long, wavy hair that was smushed in my face. I spat some of it out and leaned back.

"Aw, you're grooming me like a cat." She laughed.

"Mm, something like that." They released me, and we started for the ramp down to the beach. The dry sand gave way under our joggers, so we hurried to the shoreline, where the sand was wetter and firmer. Dry sand was good for working out your calf muscles, but did we really need that? This morning was more for chatting and getting into the local groove rather than sweating up a storm.

I caught up on all their news—Simone had gotten a promotion at the accounting firm she worked at, so she was no longer at the bottom of the ladder, and Michelle had sold three paintings in the last couple of months. She was a struggling artist but had finally moved out of home six months ago with the help of a government grant. Things were looking up. Simone's partner had been around for four months, but Michelle had recently broken up with her boyfriend. "I'm so sorry to hear about that. But honestly, he sounded like a jerk towards the end."

She sighed. "He was, and I know I dodged a bullet, but it still hurts. He said I was too flakey, and he hated the smell of oil paints."

I laughed. "Um, he knew you were an artist when he asked you out." My forehead wrinkled. "Wasn't that what attracted him to you in the first place?"

She gave me a "you know it" look. "Yep. Idiot. Anyway, I'm having a well-earned break from men. Oh, I didn't tell you! Last week, I got accepted to show six of my paintings at a gallery show in Paddington."

Simone and I both squealed. "Oh my God, that's awesome!" I gave her a quick hug. Paddington was a super expensive suburb near the city, filled with one-hundred-year-old-plus terraces and some modern apartments. There was one art gallery for every ten people who lived there, and it was highly populated. Okay, so I was exaggerating, but not by much. It was a gorgeous area, full of character, but even better, people went there to buy art. I hoped she sold every painting.

We'd started walking at North Cronulla, and we'd passed The Wall, a wall of hexagonal concrete blocks that were filled with sand and kept this part of the beach and the houses and road above from being washed away when we had storms and king tides. It sloped steeply upward from the beach to a path.

I turned to the surf. A surfer had caught a smooth four-foot wave, a right-hander. He rode it expertly almost to the shore. As he started paddling back out, he shouted, and his hand flew out of the water. My eyes widened. "Is there a shark?" It wouldn't be the first time. Not that anyone had ever been bitten here, but they were around. In summer, the shark alarm went off a few times a season.

My friends stared. Simone squinted at the ocean. "There's something big, but it's not a shark."

Michelle sucked in a breath at the same time my heart sank. When she'd recovered from her initial shock, she said, "Oh my God, it's a body."

Unfortunately, she was right.

CHAPTER 3

The surfer had dragged the fully clothed woman's body out of the water, and Michelle and I stood staring down at her. Simone sat a few feet away, shaking her head. She wasn't really coping, but I couldn't blame her. It wasn't every day she came across bodies.

The guy turned the body over, and as the longish blonde hair fell away from the woman's face, my breath stopped, and my stomach contents leaped up my throat. I swallowed them down and put a hand on my stomach.

Michelle spoke through the hand that was over her mouth, "It's… it's…."

"Frances," I finished for her.

This could not be happening.

Michelle and Simone started crying, and while I wanted to comfort them, I needed to get some evidence. The police would take over soon—a passer-by was already on the phone to them.

I quickly put a no-notice on myself and put my phone onto

camera mode; then I snapped a couple of photos. I turned and took a photo of where we were relative to the landmarks above because it was probably relevant for figuring out where she'd gone in.

After that, I dropped my spell and called Angelica.

"It's a bit early for you to be up, isn't it, dear?" She sounded wide awake, which didn't surprise me. She was usually up early, went to bed late, and she rarely seemed tired. Maybe she didn't need as much sleep as me.

"I'm at the beach with my friends. A body has washed up, and it's someone I know." The breath sighed out of me. "The police will be here soon. Frances"—the tears almost took hold saying her name, but I fought them off, only just—"she's not like us." She'd know I meant not a witch, but I couldn't exactly say that in front of the gathering crowd.

"Okay, dear. I'll be there in a few minutes. Where exactly are you?"

I explained where I was relative to the hotel, and she hung up.

I grabbed Michelle's hand and gently led her to where Simone was bawling her eyes out on the sand. Pulling Michelle down to sit, me in between them, I slung an arm around each one. They'd been closer to Frances than me, and of course, I'd been gone for just over a year and a half, so I wasn't nearly as upset. Other than a couple of tears that escaped to roll down my cheeks, I did my best not to cry. Someone had to hold our group together.

"Who's going to—to tell Cory?" Michelle cried her way through her question.

"I think it's best if we let the police tell him." I would think getting a call from someone who could hardly talk for all their crying would be more stressful than receiving a calm call from a police officer. Not that either of those was ideal.

We sat with our own thoughts until the police turned up and took our details. Angelica was about one second behind. She took a look at the body, her magic tingling my scalp, then came over to us as the police started to cordon off the scene. She stood in front of our group and looked down at me, her poker face well and truly situated, which was great because I needed her take-charge attitude. When she wore that expression, or lack of, it gave me confidence that everything would work out because Angelica was on the job. "Are you all right, Lily?"

My friends stared at her.

"I'm not great, but I'll be okay. These are my friends Michelle and Simone. They were very close to Frances."

Angelica gave them a sympathetic look. "I'm so sorry, ladies. Why don't we go back to the hotel so you can digest this somewhere less… public."

My friends, who weren't in the headspace to think clearly, nodded mutely.

Back at the hotel, in Angelica's suite—of course she booked a large place for herself and Phillip that was more like an apartment than a hotel room—she sat us all down on the three-seater couch and grabbed water for everyone. When my friends were calm enough to talk, she started her questions. "Ladies, I'm not sure how much Lily has told you about me, but I work for an offshoot of the police. I know Lily will be upset about Frances, so if I get some information, maybe I can help piece together what happened. Is that okay?"

My friends looked at her, their eyes red and their faces wet with grief. They nodded.

"Great, thank you. Was Frances a good swimmer?"

Michelle nodded. "She surfs almost every day, and she scuba dives."

Angelica nodded. "When was the last time you saw her?"

I answered first. "Yesterday, late morning. Will and I grabbed a coffee from her café. That's when she offered to cater the wedding." How could I get married now that my friend had died? Admittedly, she wasn't my best friend, but I was grieving, as were my friends. I didn't want my wedding day to be a sad one. I looked at Angelica. "Do you think I should call it off? Will would understand, wouldn't he?"

Her eyes widened so slightly that I almost missed it, but that was akin to someone else's mouth dropping open. I'd managed to surprise her, which wasn't easy. "Let's not talk about that now. You've just had a terrible shock, which is not the time to make huge decisions. I suggest you sleep on it for a couple of days and then discuss it with William."

Simone grabbed my hand and looked into my eyes. "Angelica's right, Lily. Frances wouldn't have wanted you to cancel anything because of her. Don't decide right now. Okay?" My friend was so sweet. She was upset, yet she was still kind and thinking about others.

I nodded, but I didn't speak because crying was just too easy right now, and I hated crying in front of people.

Angelica's magic tingled my scalp. I wasn't sure what spell it was as I hadn't seen that symbol before. "Ladies, I hate to ask this, but was she prone to excessive drinking?"

Simone shook her head. "No. She'd have one schooner of beer sometimes, but sometimes she'd have an energy drink while we were out. She had to get up early for work seven days a week, so she was mindful of having too much. And she didn't usually stay out too late either."

"Did she have any enemies?" Wow, Angelica was straight

into it. Strangely enough, Michelle and Simone didn't seem perturbed by this line of questioning. Maybe that spell was some kind of calming or loosening-tongue one.

Michelle took a sip of her water. "Um, her ex Craig was on her case. She dumped him after he cheated on her. He threatened to ruin her business a couple of times. He owns a café at South Cronulla." Cronulla was split into north and south, but even so, there were so many cafés that she wasn't even in competition with him.

"What café does he own?" I asked. She'd been single when I left, and I didn't remember him from before that. It was silly, but I felt out of the loop and almost on the outside. Much had happened since I'd been away. I supposed things constantly changed, and I'd made my choice to live abroad. I needed to get over it.

Simone said, "Beachside Beans. Their coffee isn't as good as Surfer's Brew, but it's not too bad. They do a good original-mix muesli."

"Anyone else give her any trouble?"

Simone and Michelle looked at each other and shrugged. Simone answered, "No one else that we can think of. Do you think someone killed her? I mean, she could've just gone for a walk and slipped. She enjoyed wandering around the rock pools at The Point."

"I'm just covering all bases. It probably was an accident, but in my line of work, you make sure you consider all options."

Someone knocked on Angelica's door. She answered it. "Kat! Good morning."

My mother walked in. She did a double-take when she saw us all sitting on the couch. "What's going on?" She'd likely noticed our red eyes and glum faces.

Angelica looked at my friends. "I'm sure the girls don't want to go over everything again. Why don't you ladies go home and recuperate from your stressful morning? Lily will check on you this afternoon."

My friends stood, and we said our goodbyes. They hadn't really met my mother before, and if they had, it was so long ago that they'd all forgotten what she looked like. I didn't have the energy to introduce them, so I let it go. It didn't matter anyway, not after what had happened this morning.

As soon as Michelle and Simone left, Angelica dropped the spell she'd cast earlier. A salty burn hijacked my eyes as sadness swept over me. I hurried to Mum and hugged her as I let the tears come. That spell must've been so my friends could answer questions without falling apart.

Angelica explained to Mum what had happened. By the time she was done, I was sitting on the couch again, Mum next to me. She handed me a couple of tissues, and I blew my nose and wiped my eyes... with different tissues. I wasn't a grot.

I hadn't been able to ask anything in front of my friends, but I needed to know. "I couldn't see any signs of major injuries on the body—just a few grazes on her arms—and there were no magic signatures. I did take photos, though." I got my phone out, brought up the photos, and handed the phone to Angelica, who then passed it to my mother. "Did you find anything?" She'd only had a quick look, but she was way more experienced.

"No. We'd best leave this to the local police because there was no witch involvement."

"But do you think it was an accident?" I was betting something happened because she wouldn't just wander into the ocean fully clothed, and I hadn't seen any evidence of her being swept off the rocks—the grazes on her arms would've been a lot worse if that had happened, and her face and legs would've been banged up, too, which they weren't.

"No, Lily. I don't think it was an accident. Unless she was drunk or on drugs, I can't see her just walking into the ocean fully clothed. And those grazes on her arms are suspicious and inconsistent with just floating off into oblivion." She looked at my mother. "Are you still up for my surprise?"

Oh, that's right. On the plane on the way over, Angelica told us she'd planned a surprise, which was very un-Angelica-like. I'd forgotten about it with everything that was going on. Even yesterday, just showing Will and my friends around my old haunts had been distracting. This morning, unfortunately, had been next level.

My mum stared at me. "If Lily's up for it, so am I."

Was I in the mood? No. Did I want to ruin everyone's trip to Australia? Also, no. "Yeah, sure. Might do some good and take my mind off this morning." It would be hard to get back into cheery holiday mode, but I was going to give it my best shot. "I'll just go and get Will." Everyone wasn't coming on this surprise trip, but Angelica said Will should come. Maybe it was a wedding gift or something? Although I couldn't guess what she'd have to take us to see that she couldn't bring to the actual wedding. Not to mention that my mother had no idea what it was either.

I opened the door and halted. A man in navy-blue trousers and a short-sleeve white shirt with two horizontal blue stripes on his breast pocket stood there. The top button of his shirt was undone, so he wasn't PIB, but he was a witch. He looked to be in his forties and was about five foot ten and skinny. He pushed his black-framed glasses up his nose, which ruined the effect of his stern expression. I did notice that he wore a police-style tool belt, which contained handcuffs, what might have been a taser, and a gun. Was he a policeman? His navy pants and black boots were police-like, but he didn't look like he was in the New South Wales police force.

A short, muscly female witch stood behind him, her straight, dark hair pulled into a tight ponytail. She wore a similar outfit, equipment belt, and stern expression as the man.

"Um, can I help you?" Going by their expressions, this wasn't a welcoming party. Did it have anything to do with Frances's death?

"I'm Agent Daniel Brothers from the ACFCALDOTSPB." He held up an official-looking bronze badge, which was rectangular so as to fit all those letters. I guessed if they wanted to do it in a circle, it would've been too large to fit in the average pocket.

Huh? "The what?" Was this a joke? I opened to my magic and had my hand on the door, ready to shut it.

His eyes widened. "Drop the magic, or I'll place you under arrest." He put his badge in his pocket and touched the handcuffs at his hips.

"What?"

Angelica spoke from right behind me, and I jumped. She was ninja quiet. "You'll do no such thing. Explain yourself. Where are you from? And this time, without the ridiculous letters that mean nothing."

He narrowed his eyes, and I smiled. It was nice to have an Angelica on my side. She was like a protective German shepherd. Okay, so she wasn't a dog. If I didn't have my mind shield up right now, I'd be in big trouble.

"This young woman needs to drop her magic post-haste, or I'll have to arrest her." His hand still rested on the handcuffs hanging from his belt.

"Lily, you can drop it. Please wait on the couch."

"Okay." At least she hadn't told me to leave. I wanted to see this guy get his.

Once I'd dropped my magic and retreated to the couch, he answered, "We're from the Australian Covert Forces Compliance and Licencing Division of the Special Police Branch. Are you Agent Angelica Constance Dupree of the EPIB?"

She paused for a moment. I couldn't see her face, but I could feel the eyeroll from here. "Oh, you mean the English PIB?"

He cleared his throat. "Yes." What was his problem with just saying the words? "So, are you she?"

"Yes."

"Can my partner and I come in?" I wondered if he'd realised that Angelica was very powerful, and now he was reconsidering his approach.

"Why?" She put a hand on her hip. It wasn't usual for her to show so much attitude—she usually did it with one look—but maybe she thought this guy needed obvious.

"We've detected a considerable amount of magic coming from this area, and we discovered you entered the country yesterday and are staying here. It doesn't take much to put two and two together."

Her sigh was audible. She moved aside. "Come in. I have five minutes."

What was their problem with us using magic? It wasn't like we'd done anything obvious in public.

The agents came inside, and the woman shut the door. They stood in the entryway, feet apart and hands ready to grab whatever they needed from their belts. Talk about tense. After a few moments of them saying nothing, Angelica folded her arms. "So, are you going to tell me why you're here, or would you like me to guess? I'd prefer the former because we're leaving soon, and I don't care enough to wait to find out what you're doing here." Angelica was on fire. I smirked.

Agent Brothers scowled. "Are you aware of the rule changes in Australia regarding witches and their use of magic?"

"I can't say I am if the changes have come in recently. There wasn't a sign at the airport." I snorted. She didn't often make jokes, but when she did, they were worth waiting for.

Brothers gave a nod. "As of eleven months ago, witches are prohibited from using magic unless it has prior approval from the ACFCALDOTSPB or it's a life-threatening emergency. Any uses of magic that fall outside these parameters are punishable by hefty fines or jail time, depending on how significant the use and whether or not a non-witch saw."

My mouth dropped open. Were witches fleeing Australia? I was even more glad I'd moved to England now. Wow, talk about the government overstepping.

Angelica hid her shock well behind a reinforced poker face. "And why would your government do such an absurd thing?"

The woman stepped forward and spoke. She looked to be in her thirties. That was too young to become a fuddy-duddy. "It's cut witch crime by 90 per cent. Soon after someone uses magic, we're on site, and they don't have as much of a chance to escape. And magic use is easy to pinpoint because most witches have stopped using it. It's made us safer from discovery as well. The whole world should use our system."

"How do you make doorways directly to the offenders?" I asked. Creating a landing spot took effort, and you had to visit the landing spot to anchor the spell in the first place.

The woman opened her mouth to answer, but it looked like Brothers wanted to take the credit for explaining because he cut her off by speaking first. "We have a unique satellite system that monitors everything and pings us the coordinates, but I won't go into detail because it's a matter of national security."

"So, how does one apply to use their magic?" Angelica gave Brothers one of her best stern stares.

He jerked his head to the side and coughed. Ha, she'd made him nervous. He deserved it. What a moron. He and his friend were about as useful as parking police. They were upholding a stupid law that was just about making money, and there was no empathy in handing out fines. He reminded me of a bluebottle—painful sting and no real purpose for existing.

Brother's magic prickled my scalp, and an A4 booklet appeared in his hand. I stood and folded my arms. "How come you're using magic?"

He gave me a haughty look. "We're exempt from the rules when we're working." Mum and I looked at each other and rolled our eyes.

"Do you use magic to dress in the morning?" I raised a brow.

Agent Brothers sniffed, gave me a dirty look, and handed the booklet to Angelica. It was like that, was it? One rule for them and one for everyone else. "You can fill out this paperwork. It allows for two magic uses per application. You'll need approval before you use those spells. And frivolous use of magic is unlikely to be approved."

Her brows rose. "Right. How long does that approval take?"

"Anywhere from a day to a couple of weeks. It depends on what the spell is. Some spells go through a longer approval process. There's a list of spells on our website arranged under categories."

I pressed my lips together. How were we going to figure out what happened to Frances without using magic? I didn't buy that she'd slipped and fallen or walked directly into the water. Would the local police talk to us? Probably not, but we'd have to try. Maybe being part of MI6 would help? Could Phillip convince them?

"Right, so this is your warning for using magic today. If we have to visit you again, it will be a fine, and a third time is a fine and potential jail time."

Angelica gave them a look that had Brother's smirk retreating. I shook my head. "This is ridiculous. Why is it horrible if a witch uses magic to clean the house or cook?"

"It's unfair. If non-witches found out, we'd have an astronomical problem on our hands. Besides, it helps the economy if witches spend money on labour. Magic means they can do everything for themselves. It makes for an unhealthy economy and an unfair advantage. We're all equals here."

I cocked my head to the side. "So, how do your parents feel about not being allowed to use their magic?"

He cleared his throat and turned to his partner. "Let's go." They made their doorways, and before Brothers stepped through, he turned to Angelica. "You've been warned." Before she could answer, he disappeared.

Angelica was silent for a few moments. Mum and I stared at her, waiting for her summary of the situation. She finally spoke. "What an ass."

Mum and I chuckled.

Mum stood and went to Angelica. "What are we going to do now?" She turned and gave me a sad look. "How am I supposed to make your wedding dress?" We couldn't even make a doorway and go back to England for a bit because travelling that far was dangerous and a massive power drain. You could run out of magic halfway across and die. Not to mention the no-using-magic crap.

Oh, squirrel snacks. She was right, although…. "I'm not sure I should be getting married."

Angelica gave me a look that suggested she was about to tell me how silly I was being. She was a practical person above everything else, and she dealt with death all the time, so she probably thought an acquaintance dying wasn't a good enough reason to call the wedding off. "Lily, I'm sorry about your friend, I really am, but if you want to get married here, you'll have to accept it will be bittersweet. I suggest going ahead with everything." She turned to my mother. "We can buy her a dress. It's not like we don't have the money."

"But what if we can't get what she wants?" Mum asked.

My shoulders drooped. Today was turning into an alto-gether sucky day, but I needed to remind myself that we wouldn't get this day back, and we weren't in Australia for long. I wasn't sure what decision I'd make, but right now, I was deciding not to mope, at least for the next couple of hours. If I wanted to have a cry, I could do it tonight. "Why don't you show us that surprise… unless it involves magic." *Argh, stupid Brothers.* He reminded me of Agent Chad Williamson the Third. At least he was out of our lives now. It was proof that good things did happen, even if it took longer than we'd like.

Angelica smiled. "It doesn't. But it does require a twenty-minute walk."

"I'm in."

Mum nodded. "Me too. Let's grab James, Millicent, and Will and get going."

Will knew I was coming to get him when I got back, so he was ready. I told him what happened at the beach and with the agents afterwards. After a brief cry in his arms, he wiped my tears with his finger. "I'm so sorry. She seemed like such a nice person. Are you sure you're okay for this surprise?"

I nodded and sniffled. "Yes. I'll be fine. I'll have a cry later."

"Are you sure?" His concerned gaze bore into mine.

"Positive."

He gave me a kiss on the forehead, and we met everyone in the hallway. James and Millicent were dressed in T-shirt and shorts, and my gorgeous niece was happily strapped into her pram, a pink sunhat on with a cute, fat, blue whale on the front of it.

On the way, Mum couldn't hide her grin. "I can't believe I'm back." Wonder shone in her voice. "I never thought I'd live to see the day."

I blinked back tears and hooked my arm through hers. "I never gave up hope."

"No. You and your brother are my heroes. Thank you." She looked behind her and smiled at James, who was walking with Millicent and pushing the pram. Unfortunately, the path wasn't very wide.

"We'd do it all again, Mum." James smiled.

"Let's not wish that on anyone." Mum laughed.

The street sign we were approaching grabbed my attention. "Hey, this is our old street!"

Mum bit her bottom lip. "Let's walk past our old house and see if it's still there."

Angelica smiled. "Yes, let's. After that, we can go and see the surprise."

I hated surprises. "Can you give us any hints?" Had she arranged some kind of flyover or skywriting message? Or maybe there was a picnic set up in the nearby park at Gunnamatta Bay? It certainly was a nice morning for it. But then again, why hadn't she invited Imani and Liv, and everyone else? Oh well, I'd find out soon enough.

My stomach tightened as we strolled up our old street. Was our original family home even still there? Lots of redevelopment had happened since we'd sold it—just before James left for England.

"No, dear. No clues." She gave me a serene smile.

I sighed. "You're such a punish sometimes." Will smirked because he knew how tortured I was.

"Lily! Be nice." Mum play slapped my hand.

"I'm not the one who's keeping a surprise from us. You all know how much I hate them."

"I can vouch that Lily's telling the truth." James chuckled.

"Glad to see you're using your talent for something useful, dear."

I gasped. "Is James going to get in trouble for using magic?"

"Oh, yeah. Am I?" Angelica and Mum had told him about what had happened with Brothers when we set out for our stroll.

Angelica flicked a glance back at James. "We'll soon know, but I doubt it. If they're tracking magic use, they're likely able to pick up the energy shift that occurs when you pull power from the river. I would imagine talents aren't detectable. Let's wait and see."

Argh, so much for a relaxing break. Now that using magic for things had finally become second nature to me, I had to remember not to use it. Not cool, Brothers. Not cool. What were the odds? For me, high. Ha.

We stopped. James stood next to me on one side, and Mum stood next to me on the other. Will stood behind me, his hand on my shoulder. Mum took my hand and squeezed. My eyes burned, but this time, the tears were for our old, happy life and all the years we missed. The devastation of losing my parents and having to sell our home came rushing back. James and I couldn't afford to keep paying the mortgage after Mum and Dad disappeared. After a few months of being missing, they'd declared my parents dead. Because of the will, James and I inherited the property, but we pretty much sold it straight away. The bank wasn't into giving teenagers loans. After paying the mortgage off, there was enough for him and me to buy a modest property each. In all the time I lived in my apartment, I never came past—it was too painful.

I swallowed. "The garden's just as nice as when we had it." Dad had loved gardening, and manicured maraya hedges grew along the front and one side boundary and alongside the driveway. One of our neighbours had knocked down their old single-storey house, and a contemporary, white two-storey home stood in its place. On the other side was a 1970s single-storey, brown-brick home. Not super attractive, but it was well maintained. Our home had been a two-storey, double-fronted yellow-brick home. Since I'd last seen it, someone had rendered it, and now it was painted a medium grey-blue, and the windows and trims were white. "It's pretty. I like what they've done."

Mum's voice was on edge, as mine had been earlier. "It is, Lily. I dreamed of it often when I was locked up. I always wondered if you and James still lived here. My memories of our life here kept me going, and the hope of seeing you both again."

James cleared his throat. "I wonder if the owners would let us have a quick look through?"

Millicent put her arm around his waist. "You could ask, although I don't know if someone wants strangers traipsing through their house with no notice. Maybe you could make an appointment to come back later?"

Angelica smiled. "I'm going to knock on the door and find out."

She walked up the two steps to the small front porch, but instead of knocking, she pulled keys out of her pocket and unlocked the door. Huh? Angelica opened the door, then turned to us. I couldn't be sure from fifteen feet away, but there was a telltale glistening in her eyes. "Welcome home."

Mum put a hand over her mouth. I was just confused. "What do you mean?"

Angelica grinned. "When you and James sold the house, I bought it, hoping that one day I could give it back to you. It's just icing on the cake that your mother is here as well. I wanted to tell you sooner, of course, but I was waiting for the perfect time, which this is." She stepped to the side of the doorway and gestured like a gameshow model. "Happy Welcome Back Day."

I sniffled as tears slid down my cheeks, and Will rubbed my back. Mum was crying, and so was Millicent. James was shaking his head over and over.

"Come on. You're all hopeless." There was the Angelica we knew and loved. She came over and linked her arm through Mum's, then gently pulled her to the house. The rest of us followed.

This would go down as one of the strangest, most emotional days ever, and it wasn't even 9:00 a.m. I felt like someone had put me in a tumble dryer—I was overheated, dizzy, and wrung out.

I took a deep breath and wiped my tears away. Like Mum, I'd dreamt of living here again, and now we'd get the chance, at least for a week and a half anyway. I held onto that thought as I stepped through the front door. If only Dad was here with us. I stopped in the entryway and shut my eyes while I sucked up the grief that came with that knowledge. When I'd pulled myself together, I caught up to Mum.

How was this even real?

A sense of peace and nostalgia overcame me, and the tears started again.

I couldn't believe we were finally back home.

CHAPTER 4

Angelica had thought of everything, and our old four-bedroom house and separate backyard granny flat were furnished and equipped to move straight in, which we did by that afternoon. Mum had her own room. Angelica and Phillip were in another, James, Millicent, and the baby were in bedroom three, and Will and I were in the fourth. Lavender and Sarah were sharing the double pull-out couch in the family room, Imani had the couch in the lounge room, and Liv and Beren were in the granny flat.

It was rather cosy.

All we were missing was my menagerie of animals, and it would be just like back in Angelica's country house. Okay, so it was also about half the size of her country house, but still. It was nice to have everyone together.

At about five o'clock, my phone rang. It was a silent number, but I had a feeling I should answer it. "Hello, Lily speaking."

"Lily Bianchi?"

"Yes, who wants to know?"

"This is Constable Ryan Brennan from the Sutherland Area Local Command. I was hoping you could attend Cronulla Police Station and give a statement about what happened this morning at the beach."

"Oh… you mean about Frances?" It would be wonderful if they'd realised she wouldn't have just walked into the water by herself. Was there evidence she'd been killed? Surely they wouldn't need a statement if they thought it was an accident. There were so many other witnesses they could've spoken to.

"Yes. I understand she was a friend of yours."

"She was." Maybe they wanted to ask about her boyfriend or something? Unfortunately, I'd be no help there.

"Do you have time to visit now?"

"Ah, I guess so. I'll see you in ten minutes. Bye."

"Thank you. Bye, Miss Bianchi."

We'd all been out on the back patio having a pre-pre-dinner drink. Will put his on the table. "Do you want me to come with you?"

"I don't know. Do you think they'll let you sit there while I give my statement? If not, it's probably a waste of time."

"Even if I'm waiting, it's not a waste of time. I'd like to come."

I shrugged. "Okay. Thanks." After his happy surprise at moving to my family home, he'd given me a massive hug, and I'd cried… again. He'd asked me lots of questions about this morning, but I didn't have much to tell him. I'd messaged Michelle and Simone, and they were going to come over for breakfast tomorrow morning so we could talk about it. They'd both agreed we needed to, and it would make them feel better or at least help them process what happened.

Angelica said, "Lily, find out whatever you can from the

police. I want to know if they think it was an accident, suicide, or foul play. And ask them to keep you updated."

"Okay. I'd like to know too. If only I could use my magic to find out." Stupid new anti-magic rules.

James raised a brow. "We haven't had a visit from that Agent Brothers guy about my truth-sensing magic use this morning. Do you think we're safe? Could Lily use her talent to find out what happened?"

Angelica rubbed her hands together. "I think so. Why don't we do a little test?"

I sucked in a breath. "I know just how to test it." I looked at Mum. "Can I take a photo from when I was young… something with you, James, and Dad in it?"

Her mouth dropped open. "Oh my word, yes!" She smiled. "With your talent, we can have pictures we don't have now. That would be wonderful, Lily. What about James's sixteenth, when the four of us were standing behind the cake, and one of his friends took the shot? You could ask to go back to that moment, and you know where to stand to take it."

I smiled. "Excellent idea."

Liv stood. "I can't wait to see the photo," Liv said. "I'm coming inside with you."

"Me too." Sarah stood.

"Okay, then. Let's go." As emotional as this was—what part of today hadn't been emotional—I was excited to see the picture. It would make me feel like Dad was here, and I was sure Mum would get so much out of seeing a new picture of Dad.

I went to the dining room, which now had an eight-seater dining table. It used to be six, but Angelica must've thought we'd need a bigger one. Considering that everyone was here, she'd been right. Apparently, she'd ordered all the furniture the old-fashioned way—on the internet—and it had arrived a couple of months before we did. Even though she hadn't known exactly when we'd have a chance to return, she'd figured it might be soon, so she'd arranged things just in case.

I stood to one side of the table, halfway down, and pointed the phone towards the end seat. I accessed my own energy. "Show me James's sixteenth birthday, just before he cut the cake."

I held my breath. The lights dimmed, and the small flames of sixteen slim silver candles glowed yellow, casting light on our happy faces. Mum and Dad, their arms around each other, stood behind James and me. We were all smiling, and I held up two fingers behind James's head—typical annoying sister. I wasn't sure whether to laugh or cry, so I did both. *Click.* I wished I could try and take a video, but that might use too much power and alert the authorities. If this slipped under their radar, I might try video next because it was still only using my natural reserves.

I shut down my magic and showed the girls my photo. Sarah bit her bottom lip. "Aw, look at you guys. That's adorable. So sweet."

"Typical you, sticking your fingers up behind his head." Liv laughed.

"He he, I know."

"Well, love, are you going to come and show us?" Imani asked from the doorway. I went to her, and she took my phone. "Brilliant! Wow, look how young you all were. Such a sweet family." She turned around, stepped outside, and handed Mum the phone. Angelica and James looked over her shoulder.

A loving smile lit up Mum's face. She shook her head slowly. "That was such a beautiful day. Look at our happy faces." Her smile disappeared. "We were so ignorant of what was coming. If only we'd known." She looked up at me and then James. "We never would've taken on that assignment. I know I've said it before, but I'm so sorry you had to fend for yourselves."

James put his arms around her. "We don't blame you or Dad. You were only trying to make the world a safer place."

I hugged them both. "We love you, Mum. James is right. We don't blame you. I'm just happy you're here now." I gave James a grateful look. "James did a good job guiding me through my teenage years. I couldn't have asked for a better big brother."

Millicent sniffled, and Liv had a tear in her eye. Will put a gentle hand on my shoulder. "I hate to break up the lovefest, but Lily has to get to the police station." I hated that he was right. At least later, we were going to grab some takeaway food and eat at South Cronulla Park, overlooking the beach.

"Bye. Let me know if that stupid agent comes around."

"Will do, dear."

The police station was a twenty-five-minute walk and in the vicinity of where we'd come from this morning, so I called an Uber. Cronulla Police Station was a small building on the corner of a busy street. The entry area was tiny. There weren't even any chairs to sit on in the waiting area. Maybe they didn't want aggro people picking them up and using them as weapons? I went up to the short male police officer at the counter. He was behind safety glass or Perspex. "Hi, I'm Lily Bianchi, here to see Constable Ryan Brennan."

"I'll just get him. Hang on a sec."

It took a couple of minutes, but finally, the door to the left of the window clicked and opened. A policeman in his early thirties stood there. Six foot tall with short brown hair, he was easy on the eyes. Not that I should be thinking that with Will here, but I wasn't blind. "Miss Bianchi, thank you for coming down."

"Is it okay if my fiancé sits in on the interview?"

He smiled. "Of course. Come through."

He took us to another small room, which wasn't surprising because unless the building was like Dr Who's Tardis, they couldn't fit much in it according to the outside. He sat behind a desk, and Will and I sat in two of three guest chairs. The constable asked me to go over my day from the beginning up until I left the beach, which I did. He took notes and asked for clarification on a couple of things. Once we were done, I had my own questions.

"I'm not sure if you can say anything, but was there any obvious evidence that someone attacked Frances and threw her in the water?"

The constable sat back in his chair. "I'm not at liberty to say, and they have to carry out a full autopsy because we can't conclusively say it's suicide."

"Is there any way you can keep me updated?" I was adding to his workload, but this was important.

"I can't guarantee anything, but I'll try. Give me a call next week, and I'll let you know how the investigation is going and whether it's been ruled a suicide or something else."

Wow, things must move slow around here. I shouldn't be too hard on them, though—they were non-witches, after all. It was easy to forget how easy magic made everything. If only the powers that be over here hadn't decided to throw magic under the bus. *Idiots.*

The constable bade us goodbye, and we stepped out into the late afternoon sunshine. It was a shame I wasn't in the mood to appreciate what gorgeous weather we were having.

Will took my hand. "Why don't we walk home through the mall? I think a stroll will do us good. Maybe we can grab a coffee?"

I smiled up at him. "You come up with the best suggestions."

We bought takeaway coffees and wandered along, checking out the shops as we went. Cronulla had been a wonderful place to live. With surfing beaches and parks, a train station, and a plethora of cafes, restaurants, and other shops, it had the best of both worlds—nature and convenience. "So, Lily, do you think your friend could've killed herself?"

Whilst I'd told Will everything, he hadn't asked this before because everyone had been waiting for us to see Angelica's surprise. He'd probably been waiting to see how I was taking it. "I don't know. I mean, Frances seemed so happy when we saw her yesterday, and why would she offer to cater our wedding if she was planning on not being here for it?" But then again…. "Having said that, people can do stuff like that on the spur of the moment." I sipped my coffee. "I think, if I was to look at the facts as I know them, I'd say no. She didn't have wounds consistent with falling off a cliff or slipping at the rockpools and being dragged over the rocks, and who would just walk into the water to drown themselves? Surely there are quicker, less terrifying ways of doing it. It just doesn't make sense. And if she did kill herself, I'll know soon enough."

That prospect depressed me. What if she'd been suicidal, and we hadn't realised? Were we hopeless friends, too caught up in our own stuff? Regret for not keeping in touch with all my Aussie friends ate at me. What if Michelle or Simone had needed me but hadn't bothered messaging or calling because they thought I didn't care?

"So, what do you want to do about it?" He was looking at

me as if he knew what I was going to say. Maybe this was his way of cajoling me rather than pushing me if I wasn't ready.

"I'm going to speak to her partner, and if my talent is flying under the radar, I'm going to find out where she was the night before her death and retrace her footsteps. I mean, Cronulla isn't that big. I could easily follow her from the shop to her flat—Michelle mentioned that she lives a few blocks from her café. From there, if she went out or to the beach, I can follow her."

"So, that's settled, then?"

I gave a nod. "I guess it is."

CHAPTER 5

The next morning, we rose at eight and all had breakfast together. Then the ladies and I caught the train to go wedding dress shopping in the city—I'd asked Michelle and Simone, but they weren't up to it. They said they didn't want to bring the mood down. I told them they wouldn't, but I understood. They were closer to Frances, and even I wasn't sure how to have fun. I was torn between sadness at Frances's passing and joy at the wedding and being back home.

While we were dress shopping, the boys were going to hire tuxes, go to the beach for a swim, then have a meal at the pub. They didn't get much if any time to relax in England, so I didn't blame them for wanting to stay local and chill. I just made sure they all wore thirty plus sunscreen because the Aussie sun could burn pale skin in five minutes. It was a lot stronger than you thought. Many a person, myself included, had underestimated the time they could swan about safely in the sun and had ended up with the blisters to show for it.

I stood in the dressing room of the fourth ridiculously expensive bridal shop, looking at myself in disappointment. Angelica had told the assistant that we didn't need her help because I had enough input from the group. Which suited me just fine. I hated arguing with pushy sales assistants. It wasn't that they were all pushy, but I was sceptical of any person trying to sell me something by telling me I looked beautiful. They didn't have my best interests at heart.

"It's not quite right. This bit's too froufrou." I touched the lace embedded with pearls that went halfway up my neck. "It's going to be too hot as well."

"And let's not forget all the food stains you're probably going to put on it." Imani snorted.

"Ha ha, very funny. At least when we're back in England, we can… ah… fix it." I knew she was right because I rarely ate without sharing it with my clothes.

"I like it." My mum had no taste.

"Of course you do, but I don't." I lowered my voice so the shop assistant didn't hear. "I'm not spending this much money on something I'm not 100 per cent happy with." The dresses in this shop started at two-thousand dollars. Mum insisted that since I was her only daughter, she was happy to spend what-ever it took. The PIB had paid her quite a large compensation for what she'd endured in their service, but still, I'd rather she spent it on something she'd get more use out of, like a house. I was only going to wear this dress for a few hours, for goodness' sake.

Liv came into the dressing-room area with a silvery-white gown with delicate lace-capped sleeves. The bodice was satin with more delicate lace panels at the side that showed a tiny bit of skin. "What about this? I think it's going to suit you."

I cocked my head to the side as I checked it out. "Hmm, I like the look of that one."

"I'm not trying to be old-fashioned, but that shows a bit too much skin."

I rolled my eyes. "You're failing, then, Mum."

Millicent and Liv chuckled. Mum and Angelica shared a look that clearly lamented the fact that I wasn't listening to her advice. Maybe it was a good thing that magic was forbidden and Mum couldn't make my dress after all.

I took the dress from Liv and checked out the price tag. I gasped. "This is three and a half thousand, Liv! I can't even try it on."

Angelica gave me a stern look. "Don't be ridiculous, dear. Your mother is happy to pay for it. Even if it's not her favourite, it will make her happy if it ends up being the right dress for you."

"Angelica's right, sweetie. Even if it's not the one I would've picked for you, if it's the right one for you, it will make me the happiest mum in the world to buy it for you." She carefully hugged me so as not to squash the dress.

I sniffled back tears. "Okay. I'll try it on."

There was no mirror in the changing cubicle. I'd have to see what it looked like at the same time as everyone else. The fit was tight to my waist, and it skimmed my hips and came back in a little bit before falling to the floor like a mermaid's tail. The satin fabric shimmered, and even though I couldn't see what I looked like, I felt ethereal and gorgeous. I ran my hands down the smooth bodice. Was this *the* dress?

If we bought this and I spilled food on it, I'd be devastated. Could I be trusted? Yes, magic could fix it if I did, but honestly, people shouldn't trust me with nice things.

"Come on, Lily. We're running out of patience, and I'm busting for the loo." Typical Imani.

"How busting?" I called from the cubicle. "I'm not quite in the dress yet." He he. I was so mean.

"You better not be joshing me, woman." A hand appeared on the side of the curtain. It was ripped across, revealing Imani, everyone else standing behind her, staring.

If you couldn't beat them, join them. I held out my arms. "Ta-da!"

My mum slammed a hand over her mouth, and tears glistened in her eyes. "Oh, Lily. It's breathtaking. Come out and do a twirl."

Imani stepped to the side, and I moved to the middle of the dressing room. Everyone was smiling or grinning as I spun three-sixty. Even Angelica's face had relaxed into a soft, gentle countenance I'd never seen before.

"That's the one, Lily. That's the dress." Liv's eyes shone. "You look stunning."

"And elegant," Millicent added. She looked at Annabelle, who was sitting in her pram. "What do you think about Aunty Lily?" Annabelle cooed and gave us a cute baby laugh. Looked like I had everyone's seal of approval. What would the squirrels think? Okay, so they probably wouldn't have an opinion because things like that didn't matter to them, but it was nice to think they'd be happy. I could just see one of them being a ring bearer, maybe Grey the Brave making his way down the aisle on his hind legs while carrying a small red cushion. I giggled at the thought.

"Lily, where have you gone?" asked Imani.

I blinked, and instead of the cute squirrel image, a red-carpeted room full of the people I loved came into focus. "Oh, sorry. You know how it is."

Liv laughed. "No, but we do know how *you* are."

"So, look in the mirror." Mum rested her hands on my shoulders and turned me towards the large, full-length mirror.

I sucked in a breath. "Oh my goodness. I love it. It's perfect!" I swivelled from side to side to check out my profile and spun as much as I could to see the low-dipping back. "It really is perfect." I peered at Mum, a wet blanket of guilt smothering my excitement. "It's too much, though. Maybe there's something somewhere else that's similar but not as expensive?"

Mum folded her arms. "Nonsense. We're buying this one. I won't hear another word." She hugged me and whispered, "Please let me do this for you. I missed so many years with you, and I know this doesn't make up for it, but I need to do this. I want to do this because I can, and you deserve everything your heart desires."

"Okay. Thank you." I'd just have to live with the guilt and make sure I wore a napkin tucked into my dress so I didn't ruin it with food.

Once that was done, we bought low-heeled shoes and a veil. And that was it. Mum had called a local florist at Mosman when we'd arrived yesterday, and they were fine to do my bouquet, a couple of table decorations, and a weave of white roses to go over the arch that Will and I would stand in front of during the ceremony. Sydney Harbour would be our backdrop anyway, so it wasn't as if we needed anything much.

We had a short walk around the city, then ate lunch. Once that was done, we were back on the train, heading home with our purchases in tow. We were coming back one night for dinner at Circular Quay. That way, everyone would get to check out the Opera House up close. I wanted everyone to get as big a taste of Sydney as they could in the short time we were here.

We arrived home close to three in the afternoon, just beating the boys. I put everything in Mum's room so Will wouldn't get a glimpse of the dress. After that, the guys arrived, and we threw together some nibblies and drinks on the back porch. Angelica sat next to James. "Have you heard from that annoyance today?"

He smiled. "You mean Agent Brothers?" She nodded. "No. Looks like natural talent isn't detectable."

Angelica's lips turned up. "Excellent."

Phillip, who was on the other side of Angelica, turned to look at me. "Lily, I have some news about your friend."

My eyes widened. "Oh, what is it?"

"I have a couple of connections here, and I've managed to find out that the cause of death does look like accidental drowning at this stage, but her partner doesn't have a good alibi for the night she went missing. He said they went out for a casual dinner at Cronulla at a Thai restaurant, then went home. He said they had a few drinks and watched TV, after which they went to bed. He claims the police knocking on his door woke him in the morning, and that's the first he knew that she was gone. Also, they can't find her phone or keys anywhere, so they were probably on her when she died. We'll just have to wait for the autopsy. My mate is going to let me know if anything comes up."

"I don't suppose they know whether her partner is telling the truth." The significant other was always the prime suspect in these cases, and I wasn't going to deviate from that assumption just yet.

"Sorry, but I don't know." Phillip gave me a "sorry" look.

I hadn't met Frances's boyfriend yet, but maybe it was time

for a visit. "James, do you think you could come with me to chat to Cory, Frances's partner?" His witch ability of truth-telling was crucial right now.

"For sure. When do you want to go?"

"Hmm, let me call Michelle. I'll see if she's spoken to him yet. Maybe we could go as a group to offer our condolences." Which would be legit if he was innocent. I'd grab a card too. If he was innocent, maybe he needed some support. Either way, we needed to go.

"Good thinking, dear."

"Thanks." I'd always take an Angelica compliment when I could get it.

I texted Michelle and Simone in a group text. We decided to go and see him tonight. We didn't think he'd be working during the day—the shop was closed when the boys went past this morning—but if he didn't want his business disintegrating, he'd have to go back in the next few days now that Frances wasn't there. I sighed. Poor Frances. She was always so bubbly. She could even make me smile early in the morning, which wasn't easy, and she made the best cappuccinos. I'd never have one of her coffees again. I blinked back tears. *Stop dwelling, Lily.*

Will, who was sitting next to me, leaned over and put his arm around me. "You okay?"

I took a deep breath and forced the sorrow away. "Yeah. Just a bit sad."

He leaned his head against mine. "I love you."

"I love you too." He was a sweetie, reminding me about all the love in my life and giving me something else to focus on. It still wasn't easy, though, considering I was about to go and visit Frances's boyfriend and her flat. It was weird that I was visiting, and she wouldn't be there. How could this have happened?

The boys had hired two Audi SUV seven-seaters so we could get around easily. There were just enough seats to fit everyone, plus, if someone wanted to grab one car and go do something by themselves, we'd still have a vehicle. James and I hopped into one, and off we went.

I looked at him as a wave of nostalgia carried me away. "This is so weird. I'm in a car with you driving along from one side of Cronulla to the other. It's as if we never left, but it's been so bloody long since we were here together."

He glanced at me. "You're not wrong. I remember when I had to drive you all around the place. That casual job you had at Sylvania MacDonald's was the worst—twenty minutes each way and more in peak hour. I was glad when you quit."

I laughed. "Me too. Stinking of fried food gets old fast. Still, it was good for some pocket money. I saved up enough to buy that mountain bike, and I had enough to go to the movies or grab a meal with my friends. It worked out okay in the end."

The GPS told us we were coming up on the building. Whoa! It was a modern block opposite Elouera Beach. She had been doing well for herself.

James pulled over and parked. Engine off, he looked at me. "It did work out in the end. All of it." He regarded me for a moment, and I sensed he was going to say something else, so I kept quiet… for a change. "Lily, I'm doing the brotherly thing here, so don't take it the wrong way. This is something I feel I need to do in place of Dad."

Oh. That statement put me on alert. I warily said, "Okay, go ahead."

"I'll preface it by saying that you and Will look really happy, and I know what an amazing person he is, so there's no shade from my end, but are you positive you want to get married? You'll be married to the PIB too, and you'll likely only ever be back here for holidays. I know you've faced a lot of danger lately, but as long as Will is working as an agent, you'll always have to worry about him."

I shrugged. "I worry, but it's all I've ever known with him. And don't forget, as much as I didn't want to end up there, I'm working there, too, and for MI6. It goes both ways."

"One day you'll stop to have kids, and you'll be the one at home waiting for him and worrying. Will it still be okay then?"

"Millicent went back to work. Besides, I'm not really keen on having kids, so who knows, maybe I never will."

His facial expression said he didn't believe me. "Never say never. Things have a way of happening."

"Meh." I chuckled.

"Well, anyway, I just wanted to make sure you'd thought this through. Are you okay with locking in your new life for good?"

Was I? Hell yes. I grinned. "You betcha. Thanks for checking in, though. You know I'm the sort of person who would come to you or Mum if I wasn't sure and needed to talk things through, but as much as I miss this place, not marrying Will and not living in England isn't even a speck on my radar. It's all good. I can't wait to marry Will and be with all my friends. They're more like family anyway. There's no way I could leave any of you, to be honest."

He smiled. "Okay, good." He unclipped his belt and got out. I followed.

Michelle and Simone waited out the front, near the security door. I gave them both a hug, and they greeted James.

Both women's eyes were red. It pained me that they were hurting.

Michelle whispered, "I texted him we were coming. I

wanted to make sure he was home. He said it was fine if we came." She hesitated a moment. "There's no easy way to ask this: Do you think she killed herself?"

Simone shook her head vehemently. "No. There's no way. Surely we would've known if she was depressed or something."

Unfortunately, that wasn't always the case. "Not necessarily. People are good at hiding how they're feeling, but I can't fathom it either. I mean, she was a surfer and a good swimmer. Plus, drowning is a horrific way to die. Who would do it on purpose, let alone Frances?"

"Maybe it was an accident?" Michelle stared at me, maybe trying to see if I agreed. Hope shone in her eyes. No one wanted to think they'd failed their friend.

I wished I could give her the answer she wanted. "Maybe, but I don't know. Hopefully the police will come up with more answers soon." I didn't want to say I thought she'd been killed. Even though my gut told me that, I had no proof. I could be very wrong. Maybe she'd had a fight with Cory, grabbed her keys and phone, and gone for an angry walk. I still didn't know how that would lead to her falling or walking into the ocean and dying, unless she'd been super drunk. Phillip mentioned Cory had said they'd been drinking. Was my gut wrong for the first time ever?

Michelle sniffled and blew her nose. "Let's go in. I want to let Cory know we're here for him and then go home. I can't seem to stop crying."

Simone rubbed her back. "You'll feel better soon. Maybe you're getting it all out now?"

Michelle shrugged but said nothing. James took the opportunity to buzz apartment six. A voice came over the intercom… a woman's voice. "Yeah, who is it?"

"We're friends of Frances. Michelle, Simone, Lily, and me, James. Michelle texted Cory earlier to make sure it was okay."

"Yeah, okay. Come on up to the third floor." The door clicked. James pushed it open and let us all walk in before he followed, and the door fell shut behind us. We got in the lift and went up.

Simone knocked on the door to number six. A man answered. His shoulder-length, sandy-coloured hair was dishevelled, and his red-rimmed eyes looked exhausted. Simone stepped to him and gave him a hug. "I'm so sorry, Cory." She started crying. Tears slid from his eyes before he stepped back.

"Thanks. Um… come in." He walked down a hallway and into a large open-plan living/dining/kitchen area. It was as huge as a house and the view…. I struggled to keep my mouth from dropping in awe. My eyes were drawn across the road to the early evening ocean vista that filled the floor-to-ceiling windows and glass door to the terrace. The light was fading, but it was still bright enough to see the blue expanse clearly. I would've commented on the scenery, but it seemed like that would be a lame thing to say under the circumstances. They must have been loaded. Apartments like this were at least a mill and a half. Maybe more. "Please, sit down." He gestured to two three-seater cream-hued couches.

James and I sat on one, Simone and Michelle on the other. A woman appeared from a door just off the living area. "Hi. I'm Frances's sister, Amy. Can I get anyone a drink?" she asked in a quiet voice. Her high cheekbones and eyes reminded me of Frances, but that's where the similarities ended. Slim and short, she wore a tie-dyed T-shirt over her huge and likely surgically enhanced breasts. Her short denim shorts were more like underpants. Her bottom hung out. At least her cheeks would stay cooler in summer.

I quickly lifted my gaze from her bum. It wasn't nice to be judgemental in normal circumstances, but since she was grieving, I should definitely give her a break. "Ah, no thanks."

Everyone else declined a drink, and she sat next to James while Cory sat next to Simone. I wriggled a bit. Hopefully she hadn't sat in this spot. Was I sitting on old bottom sweat?

Simone looked at me. "Oh, Lily, I know how you feel. I can barely stop crying."

I bit my lip so I didn't smile. How inappropriate. Also, I needed to stop telegraphing everything on my face. I sniffled. "It's just so awful." I looked at Cory. "Is there anything we can do for you?"

He shook his head. "No, thanks. I don't even know what I need right now. It's hard to think. Frances was everything to me. What am I supposed to do now? I can't run the café by myself, let alone get through each day without her." He sunk back into his seat. I glanced at James. I'd have to wait until later to get the lowdown on how much truth Cory was telling.

Frances's sister said, "It's okay, Cory. I'll stay here and help till you decide what to do. I've worked in a café before. It'll be a piece of cake. No pun intended." I raised a brow. Making jokes just after your sister has died? Maybe humour was her way of coping. I shouldn't judge. Everyone dealt with grief in their own way.

"But you have your own job down in Nowra."

She waved a dismissive hand. "It's fine. It's just the supermarket. They can easily find someone else. I'm needed up here."

I didn't want to ask any questions outright because it would seem too much like an interrogation considering that I didn't know Cory. "I can't believe she's gone. She only agreed to cater my wedding the day before, and she seemed so excited about the future with you and the business, Cory. There's no way she did this on purpose." Hopefully that hook would catch some information.

Cory looked at the floor and pulled a thread on his T-shirt. Was he hiding something, or was everything we said about Frances going to add to his sorrow?

Frances's sister saved him from answering. "To be honest, I think she was under a lot of stress. She was a trouper most of the time, but she has a history of taking on too much. I wouldn't normally say this to people because it's her private business, but when we were in high school, she had counselling for depression. I don't know that she was ever a hundred per cent okay."

Cory raised his head and stared at her. I wasn't sure what he was thinking. Was he upset that Frances's sister was saying something negative and private about the woman he loved? Did he love Frances? His stricken appearance would indicate that he did... unless it was guilt. Argh, I needed more information.

"Wow, I had no idea," I said. "Do you think something set her off?" Had Cory and Frances fought the night she died? He'd told the police they'd been drinking at home. If they were drunk and loose, maybe they'd fought about something.

Cory shook his head. "No. Everything was fine... at least with us. There was one woman, Kim, who used to come in every now and then, but Frances refused to serve her one day when she was drunk. After that, she threatened Frances a few times. She even threw a brick at the shopfront one night. We told the police, and they charged her with criminal damage."

James flicked me a glance. Something in what he just said wasn't true, maybe? Hmm.

Michelle shuddered. "I remember that. That woman's nuts. She wanders through the mall talking to herself. I've seen her growling at random kids too."

"When's the funeral?" Simone asked.

Cory shrugged. "The police need to complete the autopsy. The funeral probably won't be for another week and a half."

About the time of my wedding. It better not be the same day because as much as I didn't want to have the wedding after Frances died, I couldn't do that to Will or Mum. Not to mention we'd bought the dress, so I'd obviously decided that we were still getting married, but I couldn't have it on the same day as the funeral. Since it was taking place at Mum's friend's, surely we could postpone by a day. The flowers would still be fine, as would the cake, and it wasn't like the guest list was huge. It was just us, Michelle, and Simone. Oh, and Will's parents. They were already in Australia but had chosen to visit the Barrier Reef. His dad was a mad fisherman, and it had been a dream of his to do a fishing charter in Queensland. They were arriving in Sydney a couple of days before the wedding. Will had texted them about the no-magic thing. The last thing we needed was them getting fined by stupid Agent Brothers.

"Do you want to text me when you know, or would you prefer I check in with you next week? I don't want to add to your stress." Michelle was a sweetie.

"If you could text me, that would be good. Thanks."

Amy looked at Michelle. "I can give you my number too. If you have any questions, feel free to let me know as well. I want to do whatever I can to help Cory." She turned and gave him a sympathetic look.

"Okay. Thanks." They exchanged numbers.

Simone looked at Amy. "It must've been quite a shock for you to find out what happened. I can't imagine how horrible it was. Is your mum okay? You live with her, don't you?"

Amy sniffed and wiped her eyes. "Yes. I help look after her around my job. She's devastated. With her diabetes, she wasn't well enough to come up. I hurried to Sydney as soon as Cory called me. Mum will come up with our uncle and my cousin for the funeral."

Cory's phone rang. He answered it. "Hi, Dad. Yeah." He listened, and a couple of tears slid down his face. "Okay. I'll see you tomorrow." He hung up. "I'm sorry, but I'm going to my room." He stood. "Thank you all for coming. I'm sure Frances would be grateful that you all care so much." He hurried down a short hallway to the door at the end and shut it after himself.

"I'm sorry about that." Amy clasped her hands and looked at me, then James. She lowered her voice. "He isn't coping so well. I think they had a fight the night she died."

"Did he tell you that?" James asked.

She shook her head. "No. Frances called me that night. I could tell she'd been drinking…. They did drink a fair bit, to be honest. It always worried me because alcohol's not the best thing for depression."

She was right, but why tell us? Maybe she suspected Cory had done something? Did she want our take on it? I wasn't willing to say anything since I had no proof. But it was looking more and more like Cory might have had a hand in her death. Maybe it had been an accident—he certainly looked like a grieving boyfriend.

"She told me they'd had a big fight. He wanted to expand and move to a bigger premises. Frances didn't want to. As I said before, she was always taking too much on, and apparently their loan on this place is huge. I think he likes to live large, if you know what I mean." She frowned.

Wow, she wasn't holding back. Why come and offer to help if she was just going to trash him to Frances's friends?

I leaned forward and stared at her. "Have you told the police any of this?"

"No. I haven't had a chance. Also, I wanted to see Cory and figure out what happened. It's not that I think he killed her. Please don't get that impression, but I think Frances was under a lot of stress. He didn't help her cope, is all I'm saying."

Simone started crying again. Michelle put her arm around her and looked at me. "Maybe we should go?"

I glanced at James. He gave a nod. I was hoping that meant he had enough information, and we could start trying to unravel this whole thing. I looked at Michelle. "Yes, I think you're right." I stood and looked down at Amy. "Thanks for having us over. We appreciate it. And we're so sorry for your loss."

She blinked as if fighting tears. "Thank you." She gave each of us a hug and showed us to the door. "If you need to talk or want information on the funeral, you can always call me. I'm here for you."

Simone sniffled. "Thank you, Amy. Frances was lucky to have such a caring sister. And ditto. If you need to talk, I'm only a phone call away. Just get my number from Michelle."

"Will do. Thanks."

I said goodbye to my friends outside, and James and I got in the car. I turned to him. "Spill."

"They both lied."

"Oh. Great. What about?"

"He lied about everything being fine between them—at

least that's what it must be since he was telling us about the brick incident as well. Michelle confirmed that, so that bit must be true. Amy lied about the depression and about rushing up here as soon as she heard. He was telling the truth about not knowing how he's going to run the business, and he wasn't faking his grief. She was telling the truth about her sister's fight with Cory."

I let out a heavy breath. "I can understand him lying about having a fight with her—it makes him look guilty as hell. But why would the sister lie about the depression and rushing up here? She's here, right? Isn't that all that matters, not whether she drove quickly or took her time?"

He started the car and pulled into the street. "Maybe the sister has issues with how well her sister was doing and wanted to make Frances look not as perfect? Who knows? Amy struck me as someone who wasn't exactly excelling at life."

"Maybe she resents Frances for living her best life up here while she's stuck down there looking after their mum?" Good old sibling rivalry. "She obviously loved her, though, because she came up here to help Cory." James grunted. I looked at him. "What? Do you think there's more going on?"

"Maybe they're having an affair? Or maybe she has the hots for him?"

"I didn't get that impression. If only we could ask outright." That wasn't an option as long as I had any doubts about their guilt. If they were innocent, they didn't need me dumping that on them while they were grieving. I wasn't willing to take that chance till I knew more. It was way easier to push someone I was fairly sure was guilty. "Do you think Cory killed her by accident?"

"I don't know. He might feel guilty for fighting with her. We'll come back later tonight, and you can see if she left the apartment by herself or if he was with her or followed. That will give us more of a clue. Who knows, you might solve everything tonight, and if it turns out she was murdered, we'll have to find some way to clue the police in."

"Good point." I just needed to have patience. When it was dark and everyone was asleep, we'd return. Even if the police tracked where her phone went that night, they couldn't tell if someone else was with her. "Do you think Phillip could find out if the police have looked into her phone and Cory's to see if they were together all night?"

"Maybe. He could ask. But all Cory would have to do is have turned his phone off or left it at home, and we'd have no idea if he'd been with her at the end."

I sighed. "True. Should we follow up on that crazy-woman angle?"

"It can't hurt. Who knows? She might've come across Frances while she was standing on the cliff at The Point?"

I shook my head. "If she'd pushed her off there, she would have a lot of damage. She only had a few grazes on her arms."

"True. Look, why don't we save the questions until after you've put your camera onto it? We'll just go in circles otherwise. Besides, there might be more suspects we haven't discovered yet." Oh, great. Just what I wanted to contemplate because solving this wasn't hard enough already.

"Okay."

That night, we had a barbecue dinner in the backyard. The weather was mild. Days were low twenties, and the nights were late teens, so I had a cardigan on over my shorts and T-shirt. The sun had set a while ago. Subtle garden lights amongst the foliage threw faint illumination around the garden, highlighting the leaves of native plants. Angelica had made sure that the garden was easy to maintain since we weren't going to be here much. Mum, James, and I had agreed we'd rent it out when we left, but at least it would be here in the future if any of us decided to move back, or even have an extended holiday.

"Oh, look! It's a possum." I pointed to the timber fence that separated us from the neighbour at the back.

"What a cutie!" Liv stared at it. "It's so small. Look at the white on the end of its tail."

Imani leaned forward in her seat. "I thought they had bushier tails than that."

"That's the brushtail possums. We have those around here, too, but that's a ringtail possum. So adorable."

I would've tried to talk to it, but that would take more than my natural talent. Instead, I picked up a piece of banana— we'd had fruit salad for dessert—and carefully made my way to the fence, a little way along from where the possum stared at me, its large eyes watchful, its pink nose twitching. I spoke quietly. "Here's some banana, cutie." I left it on the fence and backed away slowly.

"Oh look, it's eating it!" Millicent peered at it, mesmerized. "They really are the cutest."

"Much better than tree rats."

I slapped Will's arm. Not hard, unfortunately. "Stop it. My squirrel army's helped out a lot lately. If they heard you speaking like that, they might decide they don't want to help us any more. Besides, they're the cutest things ever."

Will jokingly rubbed his arm. "All right, Miss Squirrel Nut, sorry for besmirching your rat army."

I pressed my lips together and gave him a dirty look. "It's

so sad you don't want to get married any more now that Mum spent all that money on a dress."

His eyes widened. He knew I was joking, but he went along with it anyway. "Fine. I take it all back. I love those cute little squirrels. They're the best."

"Just as well. I would hate to have to sic them on you." I couldn't hold back my smile. He hassled my squirrels whenever he got the chance, but I knew he was just trying to rile me up.

"So scary." He smirked.

Angelica looked at her watch. "It's almost eleven, Lily. Do you think it's time to go on your fact-finding mission now?" When we'd returned earlier, we'd told everyone what happened. They'd agreed that things were still confusing and that I needed to use my talent ASAP if we wanted to solve this before the wedding. At least we weren't dealing with any witches, so we were relatively safe. The only person we had to look out for was stupid Agent Brothers.

My smile disappeared, and I swallowed the sadness welling in my chest. I was about to see Frances, but she was no longer here and never would be again. I sighed. "Okay." James was going to drive me because he knew the streets better than anyone else—except me and Mum—and Will was tagging along because he loved me and wanted to be there as support. Everyone wished me luck as we turned and walked out.

The three of us hopped into the car, me in the back.

James let me out two buildings down from Frances's. There were cheery lights on in many of the buildings, but the street-lights cast an eerie glow through the salty air. It was dark enough that hopefully people wouldn't notice me down here. The only problem with that was that Frances left her unit at this time or later, and the pictures wouldn't be all that clear.

Still, if we could find out whether she left by herself and where she went, we'd have our answers quick smart.

I pointed my phone at the entry door to her building and whispered, "Show me Frances leaving her unit for the last time the night she died."

A figure appeared in front of the closed door. She was facing away from me. Taking a shot from here wouldn't show me much. That night hadn't been super cold, but it must've been cool because she wore a hoodie, the hood pulled over her head. I checked the windows—no one seemed to be watching. I went up to where she'd stood. Yep, that was her face. I blinked against the flash of heat in my eyes. A tear escaped. I shut my eyes and took a shaky breath, then opened my eyes again. *Click.*

One down. How many more to go?

"Show me Frances thirty seconds from when she left her building for the last time."

She was across the road, on the beach side, her head visible over the top of a small, white car. The brake lights of the car shone, so someone was inside it, but Frances was standing alone. I clicked off a shot.

Footsteps sounded behind me. I lowered my phone and spun around—that didn't look suspicious. Not. At. All. Oh crap. My heart hammered.

"So, Miss Bianchi, we meet again." Agent Brothers was dressed in his work clothes. He shone a torch in my eyes.

I squinted and put my hand up. "What the hell? Get that out of my eyes."

"I might say the same to you."

"What?" This guy was a weirdo.

He cleared his throat. "What I meant to say was, what are you doing?"

"Enjoying a late-night stroll. What are you doing?" I wasn't going to give him an easy time of it. James and Will were sitting in the car where they'd dropped me off. James had turned the car off, probably so he didn't look sus. They could still hear me from where they were, and even though we'd been told not to use magic, if someone attacked me, they could stick their rules up their ar—

"I'm upholding the law. You're looking very suspicious. What are you doing?"

"None of your business." I folded my arms and cocked my hip out.

"You're not allowed to use your witch talent either. What is your witch talent?"

"I'm not telling you. That's personal."

"Tell me."

"What's yours?"

"Tell me. If you don't, I'll make it my life's mission to find out." Man, he was pushy.

"Make me." I almost, *almost* stuck my tongue out. How ridiculous. I needed to chill. It was my job to drive him crazy, not the other way around. If only my squirrels were here. I'd get them to climb up to his shoulder and wee on him. I chuckled.

"Why are you laughing?" He frowned.

"Wouldn't you like to know."

"What are you doing here?"

"Like I said—going for a walk."

"Well, you won't mind if I follow you since you're not doing anything wrong."

"I'm calling the police. You're a creepy stalker." I raised my phone and punched in 000.

"I wouldn't do that if I were you. I have special clearance, and I'm on the clock."

"What are they going to do, arrest me? You're making me uncomfortable. Clearance or no clearance, I'm not doing anything wrong, I'm not a criminal, and you have no right to stalk me." He was ruining everything. How was I supposed to follow Frances's trail with this doofus on my behind?

"I have permission to follow you. I don't trust you and your group, and my department doesn't want any witch trouble. Do you understand?"

Argh, did I want to bother the local police? I would just be wasting their time. By the time they came here and spoke to him, and he proved he was also law enforcement—not that he could say anything about witches—it would make me look dodgy, and I wanted to stay friendly with the local police because of Frances's case. I'd just have to do this tomorrow in full view of people. Maybe I could just get Imani to stand in different places and take photos with my Nikon. It would look way more legit. "You suck. Also, you do know you're just a glorified parking inspector. Loser." Yes, he got the better of me, but I wasn't in the mood. I needed to find out what had happened to my friend.

Before he could answer, I turned and walked to the car. I got in and shut the door. "Lock the doors, please." Not that I thought Agent Idiot would do anything, but you never knew.

"Who was that guy?" Will asked. "I know you can look after yourself, but I was just about to get out of the car."

"Agent Brothers. He's following me. Doesn't trust me, apparently. Jerk." Okay, so he was right not to trust me, but this whole no-magic law was insane. Actually, it was discriminatory. They wanted equality for everyone, but what if we said smart people weren't allowed to think any more because that gave them an unfair advantage? Or what about telling tall attractive people we were going to make them wear a mask to level the playing field? They were stopping witches from being themselves and using their nature-given talents. So stupid.

James indicated and pulled out. "We'll head home for now. Did you manage to get anything?"

"Yes. I got a photo of Frances leaving the unit for the last time. Then she was across the road, and it looked as if she was talking to someone in a white car, but I can't be sure if she got in or not." I pulled up the photos and handed the phone to Will. When he was done, James glimpsed the screen.

I blew out a breath. "We were so close."

Will handed my phone back. "You didn't get the number plate, which is a shame, but at least your magic doesn't have an expiry date for pictures. That's something. When do you want to come back?"

"I reckon tomorrow in full daylight. I'll use my Nikon and photograph the girls and make it look like it's all legit. Unless that moron can see my screen, he'll have no idea what I'm doing."

Agent Brothers might have won this round, but I was going to win the war.

CHAPTER 6

The next morning, we were enjoying breakfast in the dining room, the only place with enough seating for everyone. We'd put the six-seater outdoor table at the end of the dining table. I'd buttered my toast, and I was adding Vegemite. Lavender was sitting next to me. He sniffed. "Oh my word, Lily, that stinks." He pulled a disgusted face. "It looks vile too. How can you eat it?"

"It's yum. Also, it's full of vitamin B. It's good for you. Mmm, salty goodness." I waved the toast in front of his face, then took a bite. He pinched his nose and turned away. Imani, who sat on the other side of me, gagged. I rolled my eyes. "You guys are pathetic. Supposedly tough-as-nails agents, yet you can't even stomach Vegemite."

Beren smiled. "I'll try some. I don't mind a bit of Marmite."

I made a gagging sound. "That stuff is second-rate grossness. It's so sad that you have that instead of the good stuff."

Angelica looked at me. "Marmite was invented first, dear.

In 1902, to be exact. Vegemite came out in 1922. It is you who eats the *second-rate grossness*." She smirked. Phillip chuckled, and Imani and Lavender grinned.

I wasn't giving up that easily. "We clearly have superior taste. We were waiting for something much better. Marmite had its chance, but it blew it."

Liv was sitting across the table from me. Her eyes widened, and she screamed. Beren stared at her. "What's wrong? Are you okay? I know Lily doesn't like Marmite, but it's not the end of the world."

She shook her head and pushed her chair back. "Nope. No way, no how. Nope, nope, nope."

Beren looked at the cornice she was staring at. He sucked in a breath. His magic tingled my scalp.

I held my hand up. "Stop! You'll get in trouble." His magic cut off, and I turned to see what all the drama was about, as did everyone.

Imani jumped out of her chair and ran into the kitchen. Sarah grabbed Will's arm. "Squash it. Squash it!"

Mum, James, and I laughed. Angelica and Phillip looked on, bemused. Lavender sat next to me, rigid, his focus on the huge, hairy arachnid near the ceiling.

I rolled my eyes. "It's just a huntsman. They're *fairly* harmless."

"Yes." James nodded. "They're only a little bit poisonous. And they can jump up to five metres." My lips pressed together so I didn't laugh. He was so exaggerating. They could jump, but not that far, and they couldn't kill someone. Not that I'd ever been bitten. It was supposedly painful but not even close to deadly.

"I think I'll name him Freddy. Good boy, Freddy. You keep those other spiders away from us." I turned back to the table of freaked-out faces and kept eating my toast. "Mmm, Vegemite." I was so evil. While Lavender was distracted, I got my napkin and lightly touched his naked arm. He screamed and leapt into the air, then shook his arm like a crazy person. He ran into the living room. Mum, James, and I burst into laughter. "I can't believe you guys call yourself agents. Hmm, maybe I could train a spider army too. The possibilities."

Will, who looked unsettled but hadn't run anywhere, peered at me. "You're one cruel woman, Lily. I might have to rethink the wedding at this rate."

I shrugged. "That's okay. I'll have my squirrels *and* my spiders. Yay!"

He sighed. "I can't win, can I?"

"Nope." I grinned.

Angelica looked at James. "In the meantime, dear, I think you'd better get rid of that spider. You're not being a very good host."

"If you insist." James went and got a plastic container with a lid, jumped up on a chair, and flicked the spider inside with the lid. He left the open container in the backyard and came back inside. We could grab it later after the spider had left. "It's safe to return, you bunch of babies."

I laughed as everyone cautiously re-entered and sat. I touched Lavender's arm again, and he jumped in his seat. "Stop it, you horrible woman, or I'm getting on a plane right now and missing your wedding."

"Sorry. I couldn't help it. I'll try and do better from now on." I snorted. Even though Angelica had asked us to go easy on everyone, she smirked. She was always one to appreciate a bit of cruel humour.

"So…" Imani glanced around the ceilings. "What's the plan for today?"

When we'd gotten back last night, Imani had already gone to bed, so she hadn't heard. I explained what had happened and what we were doing this morning. "So, get dressed in some beach gear, but wear comfy shoes. We might be doing a lot of walking."

"Or we might not if your friend ended up in the water near her home." Imani wasn't just being a realist right now— she was making sure I would be mentally prepared for a quick end to our search for clues.

"True."

Lavender rubbed my back. "It's better to know the truth. I know you know that."

"Yeah, I do know. It doesn't make it any easier, though." I drank the last of my coffee. "Oh, and if Agent Brothers shows up, ignore him. He's a persistent little man. He reminds me of a fly. He'll buzz around trying to regurgitate his power trip on everyone."

"Maybe we should bring some fly spray." Liv chuckled.

"Ooh, you've given me an idea. And also, ladies and Lavender, don't forget to slip, slop, slap." I waited till everyone had finished breakfast. Then I stood. "Okay, go get changed, grab your bags, and let's go." I didn't need to explain that we wanted to look authentic. I hurried upstairs and grabbed a backpack. My phone, wallet, keys, towel, and Aerogard spray went into it. If Brothers got too close, he was getting suffocated. That stuff stank. You could buy a fragrance-free one these days, but no one had told whoever stocked our cupboard. It tasted horrible too. I'd make sure to spray near his face if I got the chance.

I drove—Imani, Liv, Sarah, and Lavender my enthusiastic passengers. The drive was only five minutes, but the stereo was up loud, and we all sang along to Taylor Swift. It was nice to have fun in amongst the angst—it warmed my heart that my friends were enjoying their holiday, seeing as how they hardly got any time off normally.

I found a spot at the north end of The Wall, right near where her body had washed up. It was also close to her building. We got out, and Imani walked straight to the fence separating the path from the steep grass slope that led down to another path and the hexagonal blocks saving this high land from the ravenous ocean. She gazed out at the turquoise expanse. A small, white cloud floated in the blue sky. Another gorgeous, sunny day. "This place is stunning. Why did you ever leave?"

"The little matter of James going missing." I shook my head, thinking back to the day Angelica turned up on my doorstep. What a trip that had been. "I thought Angelica was some crazy woman. She showed up at my apartment and basically bossed her way into my life." We both laughed.

"That sounds like her. It must've been a shock, yeah?"

"Yep." I almost made a bubble of silence but remembered at the last second. Gah, stupid laws. I lowered my voice because there were, as usual, many people strolling past. Cronulla was busy every day, even in winter. The path meandering along the coast was popular with tourists, runners, and people just out for a walk. It was part of many peoples' routines. It used to be part of mine. "She told me everything. I wasn't sure what to think. How did you find out about witches?"

Imani gave me a weird look, one that said, "doesn't everyone know how it works?" "I knew from when I was about twelve. Some kids know from when they're babies, but mostly, the adults try to leave it until the kids are old enough that they won't let it slip to their friends. Some parents tell their little kids, then spell them so they can't say anything until they're twenty-one. It's just a safety precaution. It's a tricky spell, though, so not everyone can do it. Anyway… I always thought something weird was going on because things didn't always add up. Like the time Mum made a cake that took five minutes to be mixed and cooked. I went out as she was starting it, and I'd forgotten something, so came home unexpectedly, and voila, there was a cooked cake. It wasn't even hot." She laughed.

I thought about James and Millicent. "Annabelle is probably going to know as soon as she's old enough to understand her family is different. With people popping in and out of the reception room all the time, I don't know how they'll be able to keep it from her."

"Yeah, that'll be a case of a no-spill spell… not to be confused with a no-mess spell." She grinned.

"Hmm, why has no one taught me the no-mess one? It would come in handy every time I eat. Ooh, I could even use it on the squirrels." Not that they ate inside very often, but outside, their scraps attracted rats and cockroaches, and the agents at the PIB didn't appreciate rats scrounging for food when they were enjoying lunch in the grounds. Gus was feeding them while I was away, thank goodness. The weather was getting cold in Westerham as well, so he was making sure they had plenty of insulation for their little houses.

"Lily? Hello, Lily?" Liv was waving her hand in front of my face.

I shook myself out of my musings to see my friends staring at me. "Oops, sorry."

Sarah grinned. "Don't be. You give us someone to laugh at." Lavender snickered at this. Hmph.

"Well, lovie, why don't we get started?" Imani hooked her

canvas beach bag over her shoulder. "Where do you want us to stand?"

I glanced around. No Agent Brothers in sight. Thank God. "Just here on the path is good." I stood to the south of them. Back up the street thirty to forty feet away was where that white car had been parked in my photo last night. I started with my phone and turned so I was in the picture too. "Selfie time. Say 'Lily rocks.'" They giggled, and I snapped the shot. *Awesome.*

I turned around to face them, put my phone in my shorts pocket, and grabbed my Nikon out of my bag. I had a mid-range zoom lens on. I stepped back far enough that I could get their top halves into the shot because I did want a couple of pics of my friends. I asked them to smile again. *Click. Click.* Now to use my talent. I would've looked around for Brothers, but knowing him, he was skulking around somewhere, and I didn't want to act suspicious.

"Smile!" My friends smiled while I zoomed in on the street behind them and whispered, "Show me Frances getting into the white car." If she hadn't gotten in, nothing would happen.

The view through my camera darkened.

Click.

"Show me where the car went next." I panned around. The car had driven past us. It showed up in my camera about fifty feet down the road, so I took a photo from the back. I turned to my friends. "Let's go for a little walk down this way." They caught up to me, and off we went in pursuit of the ghost of my dead friend.

We stood across the road from a fourteen-level apartment building. I'd snapped a shot of the white car going into their secure underground parking, but when I asked for a photo of Frances coming out again, I got a dark SUV. "What have you got?" Liv asked.

"I've followed the white car to here. It went into the parking, but Frances supposedly left in a different car, and I can't see inside it clearly because there's not enough light. It looks like only one person is in there. See?" I showed everyone my last picture.

"Well, well, well, having fun, are we?"

I rolled my eyes and turned around, careful to turn my camera off. Agent Brothers and his female sidekick. They had no right to look at my photos, so I wasn't going to get flustered. "Yes, we are, Agent *Bothers*."

"That's Brothers." He kindly spelled it out for me. Was he serious right now?

"Nope, I'm pretty sure it's Bothers." Imani smirked at my answer. It was a good day when I amused my friends. "Are you still stalking me?"

His smile was as smarmy and self-congratulatory as they came. "It's not stalking when I'm doing my job. I know you're up to something, and when I find out what it is, you'll wish you never crossed me."

Sarah smiled. "Sounds like someone's been watching too much Scooby Doo."

I snorted and turned to my friends. "We don't owe him anything. Let's go for a swim." Looked like my little expedition was on hold for a while. We left Brothers standing there fuming, retraced our steps part of the way, and took our gear to North Cronulla beach. The white sand was warm and inviting, and sun sparkled off the small waves. I plonked my stuff near the flags, laid out my towel, and sat. My friends followed suit. Thankfully, the idiot with a badge hadn't followed us.

Lavender peeled his T-shirt off and lay on his towel. "So, what now? A bit of R & R till we regroup and go again?"

I took my T-shirt and shorts off and put sunscreen on my shoulders and arms. "Yeah. Frustrating, but I can't have him finding out what my talent is. Besides, if she left in another car, I'll have to follow her in mine. One of you could drive, but I'd prefer that James does because he knows his way around already."

"Makes sense, although it hurts that you underestimate me, lovie." Imani had stripped down to her bikini, and she sat there, her arms around her legs, and stared at the water. "It really is like heaven here, notwithstanding the spiders." She shuddered.

Liv breathed deeply. "Smell that fresh, slightly fishy air."

I laughed. "That doesn't sound very nice."

She giggled. "Okay, so I don't have a way with words. You know what I mean. It smells very sea-like."

"Well, I for one am so glad you decided to marry my brother here. We were all due a holiday." Sarah handed Lavender the sunscreen, and he smeared it on her back.

"I second that." Liv lay on her back. I assumed her eyes were closed, but it was hard to tell because she had aviator sunnies on. So reflective.

It was a weekday, so the beach wasn't crowded, but there were still people dotted about the sand enjoying the sunshine. Plenty of swimmers jumped over small waves between the flags, and a few surfers sat out the back, catching the three-foot waves that gently rolled in.

Unfortunately, for a moment, all I could see was Frances's body washing in.

"What happened to you?" I whispered.

"What's that?" Lavender asked.

Argh, I didn't want to ruin the nice bit of their day. "Nothing. Just talking to myself." I gave him as believable a smile as I could. The look he gave me said he didn't buy it, but he'd let me off with a warning glance. I chuckled and gave him a nod. My friends were the best. I'd just have to follow their example.

I'll find out what happened to you, Frances. I promise. And Agent Brothers better stay out of my way while I do.

CHAPTER 7

After being foiled by stupid Agent Brothers, we enjoyed a couple of hours at the beach, then had lunch at Sushi Train. I wanted to speak to Phillip when we got home and see if he could grab details on the number plate of the two cars that showed up in my photos, but he was out with Mum and Angelica. I couldn't sit still, so I went for a jog with Will.

At around five o'clock, they finally returned home. Before I could show them my photos, Phillip said, "I have some news about the case."

"Oh, okay." I crossed my fingers that it would be something helpful.

"They found a couple of threatening notes at Surfer's Brew. It looks like she hadn't told anyone about them. They were locked in her office desk drawer. The police had a warrant to search the place, more so looking for evidence that she might have killed herself, but they found that instead."

My forehead bunched. "Who were the notes from?"

"Her ex, Craig Jackson. They're not sure exactly when they were sent, but it must have been in the last few months because the letters mention the current boyfriend. He threatened to sic the health department onto them, also the tax department unless she shut up shop and left. He also said he hated her and wished they'd never met."

"That's harsh. Did he threaten her life?"

He shook his head. "No, but the venom in the letters is intense. He swore a lot and called her many unsavoury names. He did say that if she just left and got out of his way, his life would be better."

Why hadn't she told anyone? Maybe she figured there was nothing anyone could do. It wasn't like you could go to jail for threatening someone with a tax department visit. "Could 'get out of the way' be construed as a proper threat?"

Angelica had her poker face activated. "I'm afraid not, dear. But I think you should question this man."

Will raised a brow. "What, just rock up to his café and start prying? He'd be well within his rights to kick us out."

"Maybe we could ask around about him?" I suggested. "Surely now he's on the police's radar, they'll interview him." Would this be enough to have the police erring on the side of murder rather than suicide? It was weird that we didn't have the inside running on this case, nor could we use magic to discover new evidence. It was like trying to swim with both hands tied behind your back.

Angelica peered at me. "If we want to solve this, we need to cover as many avenues as we can. Start by asking your friends more about him, find out who his friends are, and talk to them too. Get a sense of his recent frame of mind."

I couldn't argue with that—it was good advice. "Okay." They'd hijacked me with this information, and I almost forgot about everything I'd been doing today. I turned to Phillip and showed him the photos I'd taken. "Do you think you could call your guys and have them look up those plates?" Who knew, maybe this car belonged to her ex? Were we getting somewhere?

His forehead wrinkled. "Yep. How am I going to explain it?"

I huffed out a breath. If only I could tell the world about my secret. Covering for it did my head in sometimes. "Can you just say we had a witness at the apartments?" He gave me a "seriously?" look. "You can say it's a middle-aged woman who's on the body corporate. There's always some kind of busybody or bored person who watches the comings and goings in large complexes. She can be *that* person. You can also, obviously, say that she wants to remain anonymous. Does it matter whether or not they believe you as long as we get the info?" Surely they'd had to overlook a lot of stuff in their working lives, as had Phillip and Angelica. We all knew how it worked. Bending the rules wasn't the same as breaking them, and I bet they could get security footage of the building on that night if we discovered something, and it wouldn't compromise any evidence discovered in those cars later.

"Okay, but if we find something, how do you propose we suggest the police go in that direction? We'll be treading on a lot of toes." Phillip made a good point.

"Can we figure that out if and when it happens?" My brain was overloaded, and this needed a lot of thought.

Angelica smiled. "Yes, dear. But keep it in mind as you go."

Phillip was already making the call. I smiled. He was a keeper. Angelica had done well with him.

Mum sat on the couch next to me. "What are you going to

do when you have those details?" She glanced at Angelica. "Is it time to include others in the investigation?"

I shrugged. "I'm easy. I thought that James and I could go for a drive later to follow where the dark car went that night. It might answer all our questions, and it would help me decide what to do with the ownership information. If my magic doesn't show me Frances getting out of the car, we have to assume she got to the water a different way."

"But you asked to see Frances leaving the apartment and it showed you that dark car?"

"Yes. But maybe she left another way, and I was on the wrong side of the building?" Hmm, maybe I should do a walk around it later to make sure.

Mum gave me an "if you say so" look. "I don't know about that, Lily. Your magic is never wrong."

"True. Oh, question. Has anyone been following you around today?"

Angelica and Phillip looked at each other. Angelica answered, "Yes, dear. About an hour after we left, I noticed a car following us three spots behind, and when we went to lunch, two men walked past the café we were eating in three times."

Mum waved her hand. "We just assumed it was another of those agents from that gobbledygook alphabet place."

"Well, Agent Bothers, or is that Oh Brother, keeps following me and interrupting me. I was going to see if you could run interference tonight, but it seems like they're following all of us." *Argh, so annoying.* I just didn't want him wondering what I was doing and coming up with something close to the truth.

Angelica snickered. "Hmm, I might have a plan."

"Ooh, do tell." I was all ears.

That night, we had pizza for dinner. It was such a large order that two people came in the one car to deliver it. It was interesting what four hundred dollars could get you—two borrowed uniforms and a small car with Domino's Pizza logos all over it. The owner of the pizza place had agreed to rent us uniforms and a car so we could bamboozle Bothers. The delivery guys snuck in the extra uniforms in one of the pizza bags. After we left the house, the plan was for the pizza guys to wait fifteen minutes, then Mum was going to drop them back to the store in one of our hire cars. By then, it would be too late for the annoying witch to figure out where we'd gone.

After letting the pizza delivery guys in, Mum made sure the outside light was off. I pulled my cap low and walked to the car, carrying the padded bags the food had come in. James pretended to be on his phone so he could look down. We slipped into the small car, and I was instantly overcome by the mouth-watering atmosphere of pizza and garlic bread. I stuck my tongue out.

"What are you doing?"

"If you can smell something, it means little particles of that thing are in the air. I'm trying to have a bit of pizza and garlic bread."

"How are we related?" he asked before turning the car on and pulling into the street.

"You're just lucky, I guess." I grinned.

"Mmm, that's not the word I would use." James glanced in the rear-view mirror. "So far, so good."

"Just head towards the pizza place until we know for sure."

"I was going to." He sounded less than impressed.

"No need to get snippy." I put a bit of heat into my voice,

but I was only trying to rile him up. It was unnatural for siblings to get along all of the time. I was just keeping things real.

"I wasn't getting snippy. Since when did you become such a pain in the arse?"

"Since I decided to play with you. Ha ha." I laughed.

He threw a withering look my way. "I'm going to need a holiday from you when this holiday's done."

"You might just get it. I think I'll be doing a lot of MI6 work." I bit my lip and looked in my side mirror. "Still clear."

"Yep."

"How did I get here?"

"I'm not going to be obvious and ask how you got *here* here. Are you talking about working with the PIB and MI6?"

"Yeah. I'm a photographer, James. And I'm tired. I mean, I like holding evil people accountable, but I *love* wandering around and taking photos of architecture and nature. It seems like life keeps throwing me in a different direction."

"It's in your blood, I'm afraid. Besides, you're good at it. As much as I worry about you, I'm proud of you." He smiled and parked just down from the pizza place. "Right. Let's go." I grabbed the pizza insulation bags—my camera was hiding in one—and got out.

We went inside the pizza shop, and a fountain erupted in my mouth. My stomach gurgled. We should've brought some pizza with us. Maybe I could order one now? I looked at James and opened my mouth.

"No."

My eyes widened. "What do you mean, no? You don't know what I was going to ask."

He smirked. "I heard your stomach, and that's all I needed

to know. We don't have time. Sorry, Lily, but you can have some when we get home."

"You're so mean."

"Tell someone who cares."

Argh, brothers. Looked like he just got me back for earlier.

James gave the owner the car keys, and after getting my Nikon out, I gave him the pizza carry bags. James and I went out the back and got changed into normal clothes, then left via the back door and hopped into James's mate's car. Tony was a friend he'd known since kindergarten. When he asked him to leave his car near the pizza shop so he could borrow it for a couple of hours, he was only too happy to help. I had a feeling that Brothers wasn't going to figure out this ruse. If he did, well, I'd have to allocate him a bit of respect.

"Okay, so we're starting at The Cecil."

"Did you get any information from Phillip's mate yet?"

"No, he's still waiting. The guy is in the middle of some big case, but he promised he'd get it by tomorrow lunchtime. We'll see." It wasn't like it was super hard to get information, but Phillip couldn't push. We weren't in our own pond, and ruffling feathers over here wasn't going to get us anywhere.

"Okay, The Cecil it is."

Instead of getting out of the car, I stayed in my seat. Unfortunately, I wouldn't be able to film because it used too much magic, and I'd end up drawing it from the portal. I grabbed my Nikon off my lap and turned it on. I'd wanted to use this tonight because the zoom was better, and I could use a low-light function and make the image clearer. "Show me Frances leaving this building the night she died."

The dark car appeared. I couldn't be sure if it was super dark blue or green or if it was black. I took another shot. The street was a one-way affair, so I instructed James to follow it around. At the juncture where we could turn right or left, I asked my magic to show me Frances again. The car had its left blinker on. "Go left."

The car appeared to be following the coastline towards South Cronulla and our new, old home. It parked at Shelley Park—a large green space with a playground that led to a rock pool and small beach. We'd had many a barbecue here when I was young. "Park here." James pulled in a couple of spaces down from the phantom car.

"Show me Frances getting out of the car." Darkness, similar to what was already outside, blanketed everything. A slim but muscular person in dark long shorts and a hoodie was helping Frances out of the back seat. "Show me thirty seconds from when they got out of the car." Argh, this was a slow process. Not being able to use video was dragging this out. Melancholy had replaced my hunger, and it was as if a stone sat heavily in my stomach. Frances had her arm around her companion's shoulder, and he or she had their shoulder under her arm. They were practically carrying her. She must've been so wasted.

I asked my magic to show them a couple of minutes from then, and they were blips in the darkness still walking towards the water. "We're going to have to get out." I opened my door and looked around. "All clear. There's no sign of Bothers."

"You really hate him, don't you?"

"Ha ha, yes. He's easily hateable. Wait till you meet him." I shut my door, and James got out and locked the car. "They went down towards the water."

As we walked, a brushtail possum darted past and up a tree. They were cute but at least twice the size of a squirrel and slower. Yep, squirrels were still the best.

Clouds slid over the moon, the shadow making the uneven

path a trip hazard. James used his phone torch to light our way. When we reached where the path from the street inter-sected with The Esplanade—the concrete walking track that hugged the coast—I asked my magic again. "Where did Frances go next?"

My camera led us to the rock pool. The story played out in excruciating slowness, shot by shot. Whoever had brought her here ripped off their hoodie and T-shirt. So, it was a man—was it her ex or Cory or neither? The close-up showed a stranger, a man in his mid-twenties. He had dark, curly hair, and a scar that ran from the top of his lip to just under his eye. It hitched his lip up on one side so it looked like he was sneer-ing. He had an okay physique, decorated with a dragon tattoo on one shoulder and a snarling devil on one pec. At about five eleven, he was a few inches taller than Frances. She was a slim woman, so it didn't take much for him to throw her over his shoulder. Frances's eyes were closed, and she looked floppy. Maybe she'd taken some drugs on top of the alcohol? All I knew was that she wasn't fighting him.

He waded into the seawater pool and swam across to where it bordered the sea, dragging her along with him. When he'd reached the other end, he'd clambered onto the concrete ledge and hauled her up. She'd opened her eyes at some point, and she was looking at him with a drowsy expression. James and I were a fair distance away, so I had the zoom employed. It was a bit grainy, but I could see enough that my heart still broke. "I'm so sorry, Frances," I whispered. "Show me just before she goes into the water."

He lifted her in his arms and looked as if he was leaning forward.

In the next frame, she'd hit the water face first. Seconds later, she wasn't even fighting it. Maybe this guy had given her a date-rape drug? There was no splashing. Nothing. I asked one more time. "Show me Frances two minutes from the moment she went into the water."

Her limp body was half submerged and floating further away. Goosebumps sprung up on my arms, and I shivered. I shut my eyes to stop the tears, then took a deep breath and opened my eyes again. I whispered, "I won't stop until he's in jail, Frances. You didn't deserve this."

Whatever it took, I was going to find the man in my camera and prove he was a murderer. It would be difficult without exposing my magic, but I'd find a way. I showed James the pictures. As he perused the last one, I sighed.

He handed my camera back. "I'm sorry, Lily. That was… a lot."

I nodded sadly. "Yep. At least Cory didn't kill her." That was a relief but, unfortunately, it didn't bring her back. "And I don't know how we find this guy and prove it's him without using these pictures. It feels like an impossible task."

He slung his arm around my shoulder. "If anyone can make the impossible possible, it's us. Come on. Let's drop this car back and go home. There's pizza waiting. I think we've earned it."

CHAPTER 8

The next morning, we all rose early, piled into our cars, and headed to the Blue Mountains. It was a vast national park bushland area with lots of cliffs and valleys. Dotted around the mountains were towns that formed suburbs bordering the Sydney Metropolitan Area. Sydney was a sprawling city, which was over seventy kilometres from east to west and eighty-eight kilometres from north to south, so it took us almost two hours to reach Katoomba, our first stop for the day.

We wandered down the main street and found a place for breakfast. The main-street architecture was predominately early 1900s two-storey brick and rendered-brick shops with space above. It was quaint on the one hand and creepy on the other. "This place always gives me weird vibes." Okay, so I said it.

Liv nodded. "It does feel a bit… spooky. Did something awful ever happen here?"

"I don't think so. Maybe it's the mountains thing?" I could

never work out why it made me feel that way. To most people, it was a pretty, older town. Maybe I was sensitive?

After breakfast, we visited the Three Sisters lookout and took lots of photos. The Three Sisters were large rock formations in a thickly treed valley. Think of a way smaller Grand Canyon filled with gum trees, and you'd have a close image. It was pretty spectacular, especially when clouds hovered in an ethereal mist just below the tops of the mountains.

Phillip's phone rang while I was taking a selfie with Will, Beren, and Liv.

"Phillip speaking…. Hey, Cliff. Yes…." He gestured to Angelica, and she took a pen and paper out of her bag. "Hang on one moment." He put the phone between his chin and shoulder and wrote something down. "Okay, yes." He took more notes, then handed the paper and pen back to Angelica. "I owe you one. Thanks. Bye." He put his phone in his pocket and looked at me. "We have a name and address for that dark car. The white one is a hire car, but we won't be able to get any info on who hired it that night unless we can find proof that it was involved in a crime. My guy said we weren't allowed to approach the owner of the dark car either until we had proof that would be admissible in court as to their involvement in your friend's murder."

I dropped my head for a moment. The disappointment was crushing, even though I'd known this might happen. We weren't in England any more, and my photos counted for nothing. They would even incriminate me, thanks to the no-magic law. I took a deep breath and lifted my head. "Is the dark car her ex's?"

Phillip shook his head. "No."

"So what should we do now?"

Angelica looked over my shoulder and scowled. "We have

visitors." I turned. Nooooo. Agent Bothers and his female side-kick stood about fifty feet away. He gave us a nod, his face emanating smugness. She smirked. *Idiots.* "I think we should have this conversation somewhere else."

"Agreed," said James.

Mum gave me a hug. "I know this is important, Lily, but we won't all be here again like this, so why don't we keep to our schedule, and we'll deal with this tonight? There's not much we can do right now anyway."

I sighed. "I know. Okay."

I pulled up my big-girl pants and pasted on a fake smile. Hopefully, my smile would be more genuine before the day was over because Mum was right—I needed to make the most of this time with my family and friends because who knew when we'd do this again? The only way to solve my problem of being torn between joy and sadness was to figure out how to have that guy arrested for murder and to do it before my wedding.

Not an easy task. I just hoped it wasn't impossible.

We got home around six that night, and I was pooped, but I didn't have time to be. We were all sitting out the back again. James and Will were cooking steaks and sausages on the barbie, and Mum made a couple of salads. Phillip sat next to me. "So, Lily, here's the address of the owner of the navy-blue Mazda. He handed me the piece of paper. "And the name and number for the car-hire place for the white car."

Interesting. The car-hire place was nearby, at Caringbah. The guy with the navy-blue car lived in Liverpool, a western suburb of Sydney. It was about a forty-five-minute drive away.

That was all well and good, but now what? "Does anyone have any suggestions as to how we go about this?" I was so lost without the usual benefits of magic and having the law on our side. I didn't know how normal police went about convicting criminals. Kudos to them for their persistence.

"The easy way would be to just beat it out of him," Imani said with a straight face, then sipped her wine.

I laughed. "I would love to do that. Who's in?"

"We'd all be in if his following confession would stand up in court," Will said. "Maybe we start with his connection to her. Did he know her, and if so, how? What's his motivation to kill her?"

"Thank you for being so sensible, William." Angelica gave him a nod. She was being no fun right now. "I'm sorry I'm not helping with this case, dear, but I promised Phillip I wouldn't work while we were here, and we have so much to see. I want to make the most of it." She gave him a loving look. Who was this Angelica, and what happened to the other one?

"I totally understand, and I agree. You need a break. The last year or more has been… crazy." I smiled. I wasn't going to add that I felt guilty asking anyone to work right now, and I hoped Will wasn't angry with me for wanting to catch the killer when all we should be doing was enjoying the lead-up to our wedding. "I suppose I could start by asking Michelle and Simone if they know him. At least we have his name, and I won't have to show the photo. Maybe I could say we have a description of the guy she was with after asking around? For all we know, he could be a friend of her ex's. Maybe Craig paid him to kill her?"

"That could work, dear. Good thinking. And you're right— anything is possible."

I went inside and called Michelle first. I hadn't told my

friends what job I did in England—they thought I was doing corporate and wedding photography. They knew Will worked with James, and they were in law enforcement, but that was all I'd said. "Hey, Michelle, it's Lily. How are you feeling?"

Her sigh was the heavy kind that sank into your bones. "I'm okay. Still upset but trying to get on with it. What about you?"

"Same. Speaking of which, my brother's been keeping in touch with the police about what happened, and he heard some interesting info that they're not releasing, but I think they're looking for a guy with a dark-blue car. Don't repeat this to anyone because they don't have proof yet, and James will get into trouble, but I wanted to ask if you knew anyone by the name of Emile Bannister." Argh, I was lying so much right now. If she told anyone and it got back to the police, I'd have some explaining to do. But I had to know.

"No, doesn't ring a bell at all."

"Are you sure?"

"Yes. Sorry."

"Okay, maybe this guy has nothing to do with it, then. It might be a case of him being in the area at the wrong time." Since she didn't recognise the name, I didn't want her to get her hopes up. Best to let her think maybe it wasn't that great a lead.

"Or he could be a serial killer." Worry crept into her voice.

"Oh, God, don't even suggest it. I guess they'll look at all avenues."

Someone called out in the background. "Sorry, Lily. I have to go, but I'll chat to you again in the next couple of days, and if you find anything out, can you let me know?"

I probably wouldn't until we were sure and the police had it in hand, but I reassured her anyway. "Will do. Bye."

"Bye."

I called Simone, and she'd never heard of the guy. I gave her a description, too, just in case she'd seen him around the café—his scar would be hard to miss—but that didn't jog her memory either.

I would've loved to have spoken to Frances's boyfriend or sister, but they would be sure to call the police, and then I'd be in trouble, so I shelved that idea. I guessed I should be happy that it looked like her boyfriend wasn't involved. But who was this guy, and why had he killed Frances? Had she been having an affair? Nah, I couldn't believe that. Other than the fact that she was an amazing person, she was too busy. I doubted she had any spare time between running her business and keeping fit.

Imani came and found me sitting in the lounge room. "Any luck?"

"Nope. They haven't heard that name, and Simone hasn't seen anyone of that description around."

She sat next to me. "Where to now?"

If only I knew. "I have no idea. Do you have any suggestions?"

"No, but I'm wondering why he used two cars that day."

"Maybe he didn't want anyone recognising his car near her place? It was obviously premeditated."

She nodded slowly. "Okay, that fits."

I looked at her. "And?"

"There is no *and*. I'm all out of suggestions."

I held in my scream of frustration. "Why are we so useless without magic?"

"It's not just that, lovie. We have no access to anything. We can't get a warrant and look at security footage from that building. We can't interview people. We're basically just another member of the public with no authority." She patted my knee. "Come on. I actually came in here to tell you that dinner's ready. I'm sure we'll think better with full tummies." She grinned.

My appetite was still compromised with all the stress, but ultimately, my stomach would complain if I didn't feed it, and I had enough to deal with. I stood. "Okay, you know I can't turn down food."

Sitting outside and eating with everyone was also food for my soul. Listening to everyone banter and laugh would never get old. By the time dinner was finished, I had an idea. It wasn't genius or ground-breaking, but maybe I'd find something. I searched for our guy on social media. There were three men with his name. Two were overseas, and one was in Sydney, but the photo didn't match. The guy I was looking at had to be in his fifties, at least. I showed Imani.

She frowned and stared at the picture. The account was set to private, so I couldn't dig further, but the photo definitely wasn't our guy. "Hmm, do you think he looks familiar, Lily? He could be our suspect's father. Maybe the killer borrowed his father's car?"

I blinked. "That makes sense. They have the same curly hair, and there's definitely an overall likeness. I guess I should go stake out their home, see if the killer does live there."

"By yourself?" Imani raised her brows.

"Why not? It's not like I'd be doing anything dangerous. I'll just be sitting in my car."

"Lovie, you're not going alone. I'll come with."

"No! I want you to enjoy your holiday. You work hard enough back home." How weird that I was literally home, but I considered England my real home now. "You deserve a break."

"And you don't?"

I shrugged. "This is my problem. It's not even a witch crime. There's no reason you should be involved. I just want to help my friend, and it kills me that they're likely going to say she was under the influence, then went swimming. He's going to get off scot-free. I can't let that happen." I felt sick just thinking about that outcome.

Angelica pinned me with a stern gaze. "Lily, do you forget that we spend our time fighting injustice? Witch involvement or no witch involvement, we're all invested now, not to mention that she was a friend of yours. We're not leaving Australia until we see this case closed and justice served. I don't want to have to rebook our tickets, though, and we're needed back at headquarters when we said we'd return, so you need to get this wrapped up before then. Okay?"

I laughed, but it was from a place of disbelief rather than mirth. "You're kidding, right?"

The look she attacked me with said not only was she not kidding, but she was also contemplating inflicting pain. "When do I ever kid?"

Imani licked her bottom lip. "Ah, so, lovie, what time do you want to go tomorrow?"

I was pretty sure she'd just saved me from certain death. "Let's go early, just in case he works. How's six?"

"Consider it done."

Lavender and Sarah insisted on coming along, so the four of us sat in the car chatting while we waited and stared at the modest, single-storey, fibro home. The front lawn was over-grown, and the paint on the window frames was peeling. The house had definitely seen better days. The navy-blue SUV wasn't in the driveway, but a green Hyundai was. I hoped today wouldn't be a waste of time.

I sipped my takeaway coffee and smiled. There was one positive about this morning's early start. "I think we got up too early for Agent Bothers." We'd been sitting out the front of our suspect's—maybe father's—house for the last ten minutes, and it was just going on seven.

"He's going to be livid when he finds out we slipped out without him." Sarah chuckled.

"He's a real piece of work. We'll have to think of some way to repay him before we leave." Lavender's grin was evil, and I liked it.

"Hmm, like what?" I asked.

Sarah was in the back with Lavender. She leaned forwards and poked her head between the front seats. "He's a bit overzealous with his job. I say we record him harassing you and send it to his superiors. Surely he's only supposed to show up when someone is actually using magic that's pinged on their systems."

"You're probably right." That's how he'd explained it origi-nally. "He's hated me since the get-go."

"Yes, and he's itching to get you for something." Imani tilted her cup all the way up and tipped the last of her tea into her mouth. "I'd bet you Team Turmoil that he's going against protocol by stalking you."

Lavender nodded emphatically. "We'll get him before we go. I can't wait."

I laughed. "That can be your wedding present to me."

Sarah smirked. "But what does Will get out of the deal?"

Lavender grinned. "You know what they say—happy wife, happy life."

"Ooh, look. Someone's coming out of the house." Imani sat forward and grabbed the binoculars. We were a few houses down so we wouldn't be spotted.

"It's a woman." Was that his mother? She was dressed in a shirt and a black, knee-length skirt. Probably off to an office job.

"Well, that was an anticlimax," Sarah said.

"Yep." I could only agree. The woman got in the green car and left. We all stared at the house. "Oh my God. I'm so stupid."

Everyone looked at me. Imani gave me a "you don't say" look. "You're only just realising this?" I had to hand it to her. She said it with a straight face.

I couldn't help but laugh. "Yes, smarty pants." Everyone laughed. "I mean, no. Very funny." I finished my coffee, squashed the cup, and slipped it into a small trash bag. "I could just take a photo of the house and ask to see him yesterday, the day before, etcetera, until he shows up."

"Oh, yeah." Sarah shook her head. "I can't believe we didn't think of that."

"To be fair, loves, we've been trying to stop using magic, and it's becoming a bad habit."

If we stayed in Australia long enough, we were going to lose our edge. "Anyway, it's not like we were going to approach him this time. Confirming he lives here was our goal, and me taking a photo can prove it."

"But we do want to know if he works, don't we?" Lavender met my gaze in the rear-view mirror.

"I guess so."

Imani tapped the dashboard. "Could we meet him today? Maybe figure out what kind of person he is? You could pretend to be selling religion."

Sarah sat up straight, excitement pouring off her like fog off dry ice. "Or you could pretend you're a door-to-door psychic and say something about Frances and see if he freaks out. Maybe he'll admit to everything and make our job easier?"

"Or he'll attack her and run away or deny everything and then run away." Imani gave Sarah an "I expected better of you" look.

"Just throwing ideas out there. We're brainstorming."

Imani raised a brow. "More braining, less storming, thanks."

I chuckled. "Harsh." I stared across the road at the front door. "Maybe he doesn't work? Or maybe he works from home?"

Lavender looked at his phone. "How much time do you want to give it before we do the door-to-door thing?"

Imani turned to me. "I think you should take a photo and ask to see him. We best make sure he lives here first. Maybe we're sitting here wasting our day. Besides, it's getting hot in this car, even with the windows down." Yeah, sitting in a car when the sun was shining was just asking for trouble, or at least sweaty armpits.

"True." I glanced around outside the window. "Any sign of our favourite agent?"

Everyone gazed outside and answered in the negative.

"Okay. Cool. I can do this from inside the car anyway, I suppose." I took my phone out of my bag and pointed it at the house. "Show me Frances's murderer here yesterday or last night." My magic could probably figure out what I meant by yesterday, but I was taking no chances.

A figure appeared at the front door. It was dark, so night-time. The porch light was on, and whilst I couldn't see his face, his height and build looked to be right. He wore a T-shirt, and his curly hair was visible. I snapped a shot. "He was here last night, so he's probably still inside, maybe asleep?" I showed them all the photo, then asked my magic if he'd left since then. Nope. "He's still in there. So what's the plan?"

"Should we okay this with Angelica?" Sarah was the only sensible one in this car.

We all looked at Imani because she'd worked for Angelica the longest. And maybe we all wanted someone to blame if the decision was no. "Let's figure out our game plan. Then I'll call and get her assent. I don't know about you lot, but if this goes wrong, I don't want a lecture." Okay, so she wasn't stupid. Why did I expect anything less?

"What's our objective?" Sarah asked.

Everyone looked at me. Since when was I the boss of things? I supposed since it was my friend's murder. "I'd love to know how he knew Frances, if he did. Um, hang on." I lifted my phone. "Show me Frances arriving at this house." Nothing. "Interesting. Frances has never been here, so either they weren't that close, or they recently met, or it was random, and he's a serial killer. Or her ex paid him." Cory could've paid him, too, but the more we looked into this, the more I was sure of his innocence. He seemed genuinely distraught that she'd been killed. The main motive I could think of would be money, but until we confirmed the state of Cory's bank account, I'd give him the benefit of the doubt.

"Okay, that's good info to add to our knowledge,"—Imani stared at me—"but what's the objective?"

Come on, brain; give me something that's not stupid. I hoped I wasn't asking too much. "Well, firstly, I don't want him to get spooked and run as soon as we leave."

Lavender pulled a purple handkerchief out of his pocket

and dabbed his forehead. "That's a good place to start. Argh, this heat is killer."

I was half turned in my seat so I could look at everyone, and I grinned. "It's twenty-two degrees. You'd think it was thirty-five by the way you're acting."

"It's hotter in this car." He waggled a finger at me. "Don't make me come up the front there and share my hotness with you."

Sarah laughed. "And by hotness, he means his gross sweat."

I chuckled. "You poor, wilting soul." I was enjoying a bit of payback since I'd been the coldest ice cube in the fridge over there. They were all used to the colder weather, and I was always in heavy jackets when they were practically still in T-shirts.

"Okay, people, let's stay on track. We're going to melt in this car soon. Let's just get this over and done with." The heat was making Imani testier than normal.

I saluted her. "Yes, ma'am. Who needs Angelica when you have Agent Bossypants."

She gave me a look that said if it were legal to slap me, she would have. "Cheeky sod."

I grinned. "That's me. Anyway, before you spontaneously combust, I'll keep going with my ideas. I do want to sus out how he knows her. Maybe he has friends down Cronulla way. What would be even better would be getting his name. I think I can cover that by asking if he's his dad. When he says no, he'll likely say his name, and if he doesn't, I'll ask what his name is. It won't seem weird."

Sarah's forehead glittered with a sheen of sweat. "And what are you going to say you're looking for his dad for?"

"Um…."

Imani tapped her cheek as she thought. "Not having our magic makes this so much harder. You could've pretended to be doing some kind of census, but we can't exactly magic papers to ourselves now."

"Would it be worth the warning? Agent Bothers said a first offence is usually a warning, but maybe magicking papers to ourselves would be considered too much magic use. I don't know what constitutes a mild first offence. And I wouldn't be the one to magic those papers because I've already used my warning." Getting dressed using magic was my undoing, and Mum's and Angelica's. *Argh.*

Imani pressed her lips together. "Hmm, maybe. The other thi—"

There was a rap on the car roof at the back, and I jumped. Imani's eyes widened but quickly returned to normal. She spun around in her seat to see what it was. The person walked to her open window and bent to look inside. Grrr. How was he finding me all the time?

"What do you want? Haven't you got anything better to do?" This guy was a next-level pain in the bum.

"Nice to see you, too, Miss Bianchi. What are you doing here, sitting in the car? It's rather suspicious."

I lifted my phone and started filming him. "It's none of your business what we're doing here. We're on holiday, and we can go wherever we like."

"Are you filming this?"

"Yes. Your harassment has gone on long enough. I have the right to visit my home city without being stalked. You have no right to follow me everywhere. You're scaring me." I made sure to look worried. Worried, ha. I wondered what he'd say if he knew how many people I'd killed. The only things he'd probably killed were mosquitoes and flies and maybe the vibe at a party. Not that me killing people was a good thing, but they were all bad people, and mostly I was trying not to die, so….

"Answer me when I'm talking to you!"

I started and looked at his reddened face. Imani was facing me and biting her bottom lip to keep from laughing. Lavender coughed, probably trying to hide his mirth, and Sarah, well, she just snorted. "Oh, sorry. I must've dozed off for a moment. It happens when I'm bored."

Lavender hit the back of my seat. I glanced at him. He nodded towards the house. The garage door had opened, and the navy-blue car was backing out. When it reversed into the street, it was clear that our guy was driving it. I looked at Agent Bothers. "Sorry, gotta go. Bye!" I stopped recording on my phone, started the car, and did a U-turn. If there'd been dust on the road, we would've left Bothers in it. I grinned.

Sarah laughed. "Nicely done." She turned to look out the back window. "Ooh, he looks mad."

Lavender put on a terrible Australian accent. "Mad as a cut snake, mate."

I shook my head. "That was so bad, but I'm proud of you for learning one of our Aussieisms."

"Yep, Lilyo. I'm up on the lingo."

I snickered. "Oh my God, that was terrible. It doesn't work like that. You can say Davo, or bottleo, or even Shaneo, but Lilyo doesn't work. And not everything is shortened with an O. For instance, McDonald's is Macca's, and football is footy. There are rules."

"What are the rules?"

"I have no idea. When you're born here, they seep in by osmosis. Maybe ask James. He might be able to explain it."

Our quarry turned right, and I followed. We tailed him for

ten minutes. He eventually pulled into a factory complex. He parked in front of a building that had "Smith's Fabrications" painted above the wide roller door. I kept going, then parked two buildings down. He went inside. After about ten minutes of more sweating in a parked car, we figured he worked there.

"If only I could use a no-notice." Not using magic sucked big time.

"It's… annoying." Imani looked out of her window. "Speaking of annoying…."

Argh, it was our favourite Australian. Not.

Sarah stared at Agent Bothers' car as he parked next to us. "If this wasn't so important, I'd say just drive off. This guy is worse than chewing gum on a shoe."

"Can we cover him in spit and tread on him?" I asked.

Imani smiled. "I think that would be worth spending some time in jail for."

I turned the car on as Agent Bothers got out of his. I reversed and drove further into the complex. I snorted as I watched him in my mirror, jumping back into his car. I went around a corner, did a U-turn, and went back the other way. I waved as we drove past each other.

Imani cackled, and Sarah and Lavender burst into laughter. I started laughing too. This was way too much fun. "Liv will be sorry she missed this."

"She will," Imani agreed. "That man is going to hate you so much by the time we're done with him."

I did another U-turn near the car park entry and passed Bothers again as I changed direction. Tears dripped down my face. I hadn't laughed this much in a while.

Sarah almost couldn't breathe. "Did you see… the look… on his face?" She guffawed.

Imani was shaking with the hilarity of it. I went around

the corner again. "Oh my God, he followed me." I turned around again. "As fun as this is, I'm wasting petrol, and I want to know if our guy works there." I parked back where I'd started.

Lavender took a few deep breaths to get himself under control. "Lily, how much can I pay you to keep driving?"

I giggled. "I'll do it for free after we get some answers. At this point, I'll be happy just to confirm this guy works there and get his name. I'm just going to go in there and hope for the best." None of us had a decent plan, and I couldn't wait any more. Besides, winging it was one of my superpowers.

I got out of the car as Bothers parked next to me. Ignoring him, I strode to the fabrication business. The entry office contained a desk that looked to be from the 1970s. The walls were an off-white colour, and there were a couple of pictures of engineering drawings on the walls. A door led into what looked like the factory part.

I dinged the silver bell on the table. Well, it was my lucky day… notwithstanding Bothers doing what he did best. The person I wanted to see walked through from the factory.

"Hello, can I help you?" He wore a pair of coveralls, which must've been worse than sitting in my car heat-wise. I doubted the factory had air conditioning either. Did I feel sorry for him? Yeah, nah.

I made a surprised face. "Oh, I know you! Fancy seeing you here." I slapped my forehead. "Oh my God. I'm so embarrassed. I can't remember your name. I know your last name is Cannister…, no! Bannister!" I pointed at him enthusiastically as if I'd just reinvented the wheel. "I'm so sorry that I can't remember your first name. I'm Hayley. What's your name again?"

He stared at me, not sure what to make of me if his lack of

expression was anything to go by. "Fabian. I have to say, though. I don't remember you. Are you sure you know me?"

"Yes, for sure. I knew your last name, didn't I? Well, on the second guess. I can't remember where I know you from, though." I cocked my head to the side. "Hmm, I go out in the city sometimes. Maybe there?"

He shrugged. "Maybe. So, what can I help you with?" He glanced back into the workshop. He probably had work to get done, which suited me fine.

"Ah, I'm getting married soon, and I was wondering if you guys could fabricate a steel bed that looks kind of like a Decepticon? But I need it to be ready in two weeks. My fiancé's favourite is Optimus Prime, but I guess he's everyone's favourite." I smiled and gave him my best "no one is home right now, please call back later" look.

He frowned. "I'm sorry, but no. We don't make furniture."

"Can you recommend anywhere that might?"

He scratched his head. "Look, to be honest, I doubt anywhere does, and not in two weeks. Look, sorry I can't help, but I gotta get back to work." He turned and re-entered the factory part. I smiled. I got what I came for.

Now to do something with it.

CHAPTER 9

W e drove home after I spoke to Fabian. I made sure to play with Bothers on the way. I drove around one roundabout four times, which had us all in hysterics again. I slowed down at an orange light, then sped through it, losing him for the rest of the drive. I was rather proud of myself. Even though he'd eventually figure out I'd gone home, it was fun messing with him.

Once we got back, the four of us searched the internet for any social media accounts of Fabian's. We found two. The first was an Instagram account, which just had pictures of what looked like his dog, a few photos from nightclubs, and fancy bars full of colourful bottles in the background. His Facebook account was private, like his father's.

Bummer. "Nothing that ties him to Frances, Cory, or Craig. I don't even recognise any of those clubs. They're not around Cronulla."

"Frances could've gone out other places." Sarah was right, of course.

"True, but she loved the vibe around here, and most of her mates went out around here; at least that's what happened back when I lived here. I used to see her out all the time. And now she owns the café, I would imagine she wouldn't have wanted late nights. We could ask her partner?"

"No, we can't," Imani said. "He'd wonder why we were asking. It's a weird question. We can't exactly explain we think she's been murdered, and we're looking into it. He might ask questions, and we have no answers. It's almost like we'd be torturing him."

"Argh, why is this so hard?" I was ready to tear my hair out, literally. "I guess I could ask Michelle and Simone." I hated bothering them and reminding them, but they knew I was trying to help, and they wanted to pitch in too. It stopped us all feeling helpless. I called Michelle. "Hey, how's it going?" It was a stupid question because of course she'd be sad, and I hated asking it, but how could I not? There were no good options in this case. Texting was easier, but I had too much to say.

"Hey. You know. Surviving. What about you?"

"I'm okay. I was looking into things this morning, and I was wondering if Frances used to go out in the city or somewhere outside the Shire? Did you guys go further afield much?"

"Not really. The last time we went into the city was about three months ago. To be honest, since she's been working all weekend and with her new guy, she doesn't close it down anymore. We were lucky to see her out a couple of times a month lately."

"Oh, okay. Thanks."

"So, why the question? What have you found out?" The

hope in her voice cut me clean through. I wished I could tell her everything.

"Not much. We might have a lead, but I can't say anything because I have no proof, and I don't have a motive." I licked my lips and held back from biting my nails. "Um, do you think Frances was capable of cheating on Cory?"

"No. No way." Well, there was no hesitation there. "You knew her. Do you really think she'd do that?"

"I wouldn't think so, but then, how much do we really know people? I mean, she ran out the other night. Maybe they haven't been getting along?"

"Not from what I've seen. They had the occasional spat, but who doesn't? He's always good to her. Bought her flowers and took her to dinner for her birthday, they surf together. I'm pretty sure they were getting along. Do you think it could be a random crime? Is this person a serial killer? And I know we feel like she couldn't have killed herself, but do you have proof?"

"I don't know. That's what I'm trying to find out. Frances committing suicide is, in my mind, still an unlikely option. This afternoon, I looked for deaths in the last few months, and there wasn't anything, although a couple of women her age have gone missing in that time in Sydney, but that doesn't mean anything." People went missing for many reasons, and sometimes, they weren't dead. I couldn't really tie anything like that to this murder. "Try not to worry. Serial killers are rare. I'm betting there's a clue somewhere that will prove that Frances didn't kill herself and that a particular person killed her for a particular reason."

"Okay. I'm still going to freak out a bit. Anyway, if you have any other questions, feel free to call me."

"Okay. Thanks. And if you're worried, call me. I'm sure we could rustle up another bed in our house."

"Thanks. You're the best." I heard the smile in her voice. "Catch up for a coffee before the wedding?"

"Yes, for sure. If only you didn't have to work while I was here." Life didn't stop for everyone because I was in town.... Hmm, not counting Frances. How depressing. Why did my brain have to go there?

"Bills to pay, etcetera, etcetera. Take care, Lily, and let me know if you come up with anything."

"I will. Love you, lady."

"Love you too. Good luck. Bye."

My friends were looking at me expectantly. "Nope. She doesn't think she'd have an affair. Do you think this was random?" If it was, this guy could strike again. That made things even more urgent. As much as I'd tried to reassure Michelle, I was trying to reassure myself that there was a connection. There was no way I could leave this country without seeing him arrested.

Maybe I'd have to break the law to do it.

Lavender patted my shoulder. "Like you said to your friend —serial killers are rare. And why would she get in the car with him in the first place?"

"I don't know. Maybe she was angry and drunk and thought it was a good idea at the time?" I hugged myself. If only she hadn't gotten into that car. "Why do you think he changed cars?"

Imani answered, "That's easy. If anyone saw her getting into that car, they wouldn't link it to the other car. Although, you would think he should've used the white car both times because someone could've seen him with her at the beach, and now there's likely DNA in his car."

I knew we were supposed to be on holiday, but this whole thing was consuming me. "I want to stake out his place. Something's gotta turn up. What are we missing?"

Sarah and Lavender shared a concerned look. Sarah's voice was gentle. "You know you don't have to solve this. Maybe we can write a letter to the police or something. Give them an anonymous tip that we saw him with Frances at the beach. That might give them probable cause to search the car."

"But wouldn't they need a witness to stand up in court and confirm that so they can use that evidence? There's no way I can do that. I'm Frances's friend. They'd never believe me."

"Hmm." Imani had her thinking look activated. "But if they had probable cause, they could possibly check traffic camera footage, and if his car was in the area, wouldn't that be enough?"

Sarah cocked her head to the side. "I don't know. If he doesn't have someone to lie about an alibi, possibly. But if he has an alibi, I don't know that they'd be able to look at footage. And I'm not sure how it works if only one source gives anonymous info that doesn't match something else they already know about."

Lavender stood. "All we can do is try. But now isn't the time to think about it. It might only be the middle of the afternoon in Sydney, but it's late at night somewhere in the world, and I'm going to get a refreshment. Does anyone want one?"

Sarah smirked. "By refreshment, do you mean wine?"

He grinned and threw his hands in the air. "Guilty as charged! So, who wants wine?" We all put our hands up. "Let's get this party started. It can be the pre-pre-pre-pre-hen's-night hen's night." I was pretty sure there should've been a couple more "pres" in there. Plus, Will would be home soon, but I wasn't going to argue. A drink—or three—was just what I needed. Wine o'clock had officially begun.

CHAPTER 10

The next day was sunny again. Living in Westerham, I'd missed our delightful weather. Not that it never rained, but our default setting was sunny, although we did have to deal with humidity. I guessed nowhere was perfect.

First thing in the morning, we discussed our idea to tip off the police. Phillip confirmed it wouldn't lead to them doing anything unless they had prior information to go off that would align with our tip. I shook off the sinking feeling that we'd never get this guy, because we were having a group outing today, and I wasn't going to ruin it for anyone. Besides, I knew Frances would hate that I was obsessing over this. She'd want me to enjoy my holiday too.

We'd gone into the city, hopped on a ferry at Circular Quay, and come across to Manly for lunch. We were watching the surfers at Manly Beach. Beren shook his head. "How many gorgeous beaches do you guys have in just one city?"

I smiled. "A lot. Sydney really is stunning, but it doesn't have the history and atmosphere of London."

"Atmosphere, shmatmosphere." Liv looked at me. "I can't believe you chose us over this. Besides, half our atmosphere is because of pollution." She giggled.

I gave her a hug. "I'd choose you guys over this every day of the week, pollution or no pollution." I let her go. "Don't get me wrong—I love my home city—but something was always missing."

Will lowered his voice. "That might have just been the magic… or me."

"Or me and Mum." James winked.

I chuckled. "Or maybe it was the squirrels. Yep, that's what it was. How could I not realise earlier?" All jokes aside, Sydney would be perfect if it had squirrels. I missed my fluffy buttheads.

"Thanks, Lily. Despite this proclamation, I'll marry you anyway. I'm a sucker for punishment." Will slid his arm around my waist and kissed my forehead.

"You're also super lucky. Don't forget that." I gave him a cheeky grin, and he laughed. I'd promised Will that today I wouldn't think about Frances's murder. Every time my brain went there, I redirected it. It wasn't easy, but we all deserved this time together to be happy. When I thought of everything we'd been through the last year and a half, it hit home that it was a miracle we were all still alive and here together. I breathed the sea air into my nose and shut my eyes, appreciating the moment.

My stomach grumbled, breaking the peaceful spell.

Angelica, who wasn't even standing next to me, smirked. "It's not even twelve o'clock. Didn't you just have breakfast?"

"Breakfast was hours ago. My stomach isn't unreasonable."

"Why don't we find somewhere for lunch," Mum said. "That way we'll be sure to get a table that fits all of us."

"Hear, hear." Lavender rubbed his stomach. "I was a bit seedy for breakfast this morning. I could do with some sustenance and maybe another refreshment."

"Hair of the dog?" James gave Lavender a knowing look. When everyone else had gotten home early evening, we were already two sheets to the wind, but Lavender had been the worst of us. I stopped drinking about that time because I didn't want a hangover. Will, Beren, and Liv had a few drinks, too, and it had been a great night. Our late night probably hadn't helped Lavender's health, either, because it was after one when we all said goodnight, and we'd gotten up earlyish to hop on the train this morning.

"Something like that." He grimaced.

Angelica gave him a serene smile. "Why don't we put you out of your misery, then? Shame we don't have magic to deal with this."

Mum frowned. "The new laws are ridiculous. And why is that weasel still following us?"

I turned to where Mum was looking, and sure enough, there he was. *Argh.* I got my phone out and filmed. "Agent Bothers—his name is Brothers, but he keeps bothering us. Why is he following us around? It's not his job to harass tourists, is it? He hasn't left us alone since the second day we were here. This is unacceptable."

"What are you going to do, Lily? Put it on Tiktok?" Beren asked.

I smiled. "Nope. I'm compiling a record of all the times he follows us to prove harassment. He has no reason to follow us everywhere. Does he follow every other… one of our kind around the place every day? I doubt that very much. He has it in for us for some reason."

Angelica narrowed her eyes at him. "I'll make some calls later. You're right, dear. This is entirely unacceptable." She raked her gaze over all of us. "Let's not allow him to ruin our day. Ignore him. Let's go."

We had lunch at a great Italian place, went for another walk around, then hopped on the ferry. We strolled around to the Opera House, had a drink at the Opera Bar, and then dinner at Circular Quay. The harbourside was brimming with chatting crowds, the atmosphere happy and energised. The Harbour Bridge and city twinkled with colourful lights in the near distance. Ah, this was the life.

After dessert, we trained it home. We were all happily exhausted when we got back close to ten and plonked onto the couches in the lounge room. "Anyone want a tea or coffee?"

"Mum, aren't you tired?" I stood. There was no way I was going to let her do it all by herself. How had I taken so long to get used to using magic for everything? It really was incredible, and now we had to do everything the hard way.

"Sit down, sweetie. It's fine. I'm used to it." She smiled, but I could see the sadness behind it. She hadn't wanted to try and get her magic back because she was scared of it never happening, so she just ignored the whole thing. That was something I needed to work on when we returned home. I figured I'd hit Beren up and see what we could come up with. Something was burned out inside her, and since Beren was our best healer, I figured our greatest chance lay in us working together. I hadn't told Mum because it was a sore spot... no pun intended.

"But if I'm exhausted, you must be even worse."

She gave me a stern look. "Are you suggesting I'm too old

and I couldn't possibly be okay to make a few cups of tea after being out all day?"

James smirked at me. I pressed my lips together to stop my smile. "Never. Would I be so stupid?"

Mum raised a brow. "Yes. Now sit. I want to. This is my home, and I always did enjoy entertaining."

Angelica and Millicent shared a look, then stood. "We'll help," Millicent said. "Besides, I need to get missy her bottle." Annabelle giggled. She'd napped on the train on the way home, so she was ready for action, even though this was way past her bedtime. James was on the floor with her, making her soft-toy bunny bounce around. She thought it was the best.

"So, who wants what? We haven't got all night." Angelica didn't muck around. We all said what we'd like, and she, Mum, and Millicent disappeared into the kitchen.

My phone rang. "Lily, you're not going to believe this." Michelle sounded out of breath.

"What? What happened?"

"I was over visiting Amy this evening, and the police called Cory. They told him they found alcohol and a sedative in Frances's system, diazepam, and they're ruling accidental drowning and have closed the case. He wanted to know if I'd given them to her. He was so upset. I've never even taken Valium or anything before. I don't have that stuff around here."

So, that was what that jerk had given her that had made her so pliable. "Oh, wow. That's not good. Did he call Simone too?"

"I don't know. She went to her brother's place. I haven't called her yet."

"I'll text Simone. Thanks for telling me. Are you okay? Do you want some company?"

She blew out a loud breath. "No, it's fine. I'm going to have a wine, watch *Rizzoli & Isles*, and go to bed."

"Okay. Call me if you need anything."

"Will do. Bye."

"Bye." I relayed the information to my friends. This would mean the police weren't going to chase up any other avenues. The murderer was going to get away with it if we couldn't figure out how to expose them.

Will gave me a look. "We're not talking about this today, remember?"

"But that guy is going to get away with it! Besides, it's almost tomorrow, and *she* called *me*. That's hardly my fault."

"No, it's not, but we'll get back to it tomorrow. Okay? There's nothing we can do right this moment, or in the next few hours. The killer will still be there in the morning." He gave me a hopeful look.

I pouted and sank into the couch. "Okay." My gut churned with anger and frustration. I was not going to let this go until that piece of poo was in jail.

Will put his arm around me. "You deserve a holiday, too, you know. I hate that this happened, and I'm sorry about your friend, but I care more about you than what happened. You care about everyone and everything too much sometimes."

"How can you care *too much*?"

"When you can't even go for a two-week holiday with your loved ones because you're going to get married, and you still get involved rather than leaving it to the local police." I opened my mouth to say something, and he put his finger over my lips. "No arguing. Just today. Okay?"

I nodded, then sucked his finger into my mouth and bit it.

"Ouch!" He pulled his finger out and shook his hand.

I laughed. "It wasn't that hard."

"It was."

"Is there blood?"

He looked at it. "No."

"Well, then, it's just a harmless nip."

"You're becoming more and more like a feral squirrel every day." Lavender laughed. "Who wants to play cards?"

We all put our hands up. My friends were awesome, helping me put aside my worries. Tonight, I'd enjoy everything, and tomorrow would be… well, tomorrow. There was plenty of time to figure this out then.

CHAPTER 11

The next morning at breakfast, I received an unexpected call. "Hello, Lily speaking."

"Hi, Lily. I got your number from Michelle. It's Amy, Frances's sister."

"Oh, hello. How are you?" I couldn't imagine how difficult this was for her to just get on with things, especially since the date for the funeral hadn't even been confirmed. It probably wouldn't be long now that the coroner had released their findings.

"I'm upset, but life goes on, and I know Frances would want me and Cory to make sure the café didn't go down the toilet. Which is why I'm calling you." She paused. "I wanted to do a social media blast about how we're open and we hope people will come and support us after the devastating passing of Frances. Michelle mentioned you were a photographer. I was wondering if you could come down today and take some photos for us? I know it's a lot to ask on short notice, but—"

"No, no, of course I can come. What time do you want me there?" At least this was something I could do to help.

"It's ten to nine now. Do you think you could be here by nine thirty?"

"Yeah, sure. See you then."

"Thanks, Lily. You're a lifesaver. Frances always told me how awesome her friends were, and I'm glad she was right. Bye."

"Bye." How amazing that Amy was doing her best to continue her sister's dream. It was also good of her to help Cory out. I supposed she'd be inheriting Frances's share of the café, which, from what my friends had said was the majority share. Would she keep it and continue her sister's dream, or would she sell to Cory? How did any of this play into the killer's hands? Was her ex trying to get rid of the competition, or did he just hate seeing her succeed? If it wasn't her ex behind all this, then who? I still couldn't work out how Cory could benefit, unless he was having an affair and wanted her out of the way. I sighed. These were heavy thoughts for the first thing in the morning.

"Lily, I said, who was that?" Imani was waving her hand in front of my face.

I did a double-take. "Oh, sorry. That was Amy, Frances's sister. She needs me down at the café this morning to take some promotional photos. They're going to do some posts to tell everyone that they're open for business."

"Don't forget, Lily, we have the cake tasting later today. We have to decide the final flavour." Mum grabbed another fried egg and put it on her plate.

"Of course I won't forget. Two o'clock at Angel Cakes."

James spooned food into Annabelle's mouth. "Why are you tasting cakes? We all know you want quadruple chocolate."

I gave him a withering look. "There's no such thing as quadruple chocolate. Although, there should be. Besides, we have to make sure it's good. I might have two different flavours so there's something for anyone who doesn't want chocolate." I would've had three, but there weren't that many of us, so we weren't going to get a ginormous cake… unfortunately.

Will turned to me. "Tell the truth, Lily. You don't care about having two flavours."

I innocently glanced around. "What?"

James gave me a knowing look. "Yes, Lily. Fess up. I know you're lying."

I gave him the side-eye. "Argh, fine. I just want to eat cake. Happy now? Seriously, you'd think it was a crime."

"Leave your sister alone, James. She loves her cake, and I want her to be happy. Every bride gets to sample cakes. It's the best part of the wedding planning… except for seeing her in that dress." Mum's eyes glistened.

Millicent rubbed Mum's back. "You're a good mum. The wedding's going to be perfect."

I smiled. "It really is." I grabbed Will's hand and stared into his gorgeous grey-blues. "I can't wait to marry you."

He smiled. "Just as well. The suit hire isn't refundable."

My mouth dropped open, and everyone laughed. I took my hand back and swatted his arm. "You're such a meanie."

He waggled his brows. "Gotta keep you on your toes."

"Speaking of which" I looked at my phone—"I'd best get dressed and get going. Who wants to come for a walk to Frances's café?"

Will, Liv, Imani, and Beren voiced their yeses. We each washed our dishes, dried them, and put them away—I did not miss this manual labour stuff—and got ready. We were out the door in ten minutes.

"Another perfect day," said Beren. "Does it ever rain?"

"Of course it does." I pointed to the grass next to the footpath. "Look, grass. We do have droughts every now and then. There was a really bad year where everyone's gardens died, and the lawns were all brown. We weren't allowed to water anything or wash our cars. That was pretty bad." We hadn't quite run out of water, but just in case it happened again and was worse, they'd spent billions building a desalination plant that we actually hadn't needed since. At least it was there if there was a next time.

Chatting and walking in the morning sunshine, it hit me—I was free. I'd spent so long being holed up in one of Angelica's houses and then the other with no fun outings that I'd forgotten what it was like just to stroll around and enjoy the scenery. Being hunted by the directors and their affiliated crime gangs had stifled all our lives, and when we'd finally dealt with them, we'd come straight here. I hadn't had time to just enjoy my newfound freedom with Frances's murder happening as soon as we arrived. But now I remembered, and I appreciated the moment.

"What are you smiling about?" Will asked.

"No one's after us… well, except that idiot from the alphabet-soup anti-magic place. We're free to walk around, go where we want, and no one's going to attempt to kill us. It's refreshing."

Beren chuckled. "Refreshing, indeed. It is rather nice, isn't it?"

We soon arrived at the café. A crowd had gathered, and there were a few bunches of flowers and a pile of cards on one table. A couple of women were chatting and had tears in their eyes. Frances's customers cared about her, and she was going to be sorely missed. Cory and Amy were making coffees, and another employee was manning the cash register. Amy was chatting with customers, but Cory wasn't saying much. His grim expression said everything he was thinking. If I'd known him better, I would've given him a hug. He truly looked devastated. It made me think there was no way he could be involved in Frances's murder. I also couldn't figure out what he stood to gain since he would have to buy out Frances's share anyway… well, if the will had left it to her sister. Maybe Frances had left it to him? Hmm…. We really needed to find out what was in her will.

"Lily!" Simone stood next to me and gave me a hug. She must've been able to come down because it was Saturday.

"Hey, lady. How are you?"

"I'm okay. Getting there." At least she looked like she'd stopped crying. "Are you here to take the photos?"

"Yep. Amy said Michelle suggested me."

"We both did. Amy's really nice. She had us over for dinner last night. She said she wanted to spend time with people who knew her sister well, so we could talk about the good times and give her more memories about her sister."

"How nice. How's Cory, though? Is she still staying at his place?" The way he looked today, I didn't think he'd want to talk about Frances non-stop.

"She is. Cory's been depressed. He had dinner with us but then excused himself and went to bed. That's when Amy mentioned the café and did we know anyone who could take some professional photos. I hope you don't mind." She bit her bottom lip.

I smiled. "Of course not! I'm only too happy to help. Cory's going through enough by the sounds of it. If I can make his life easier, I'm there."

She squeezed my hand. "You're the best, Lily. Michelle and I have really missed you."

"I've missed you guys too."

Amy had hurried out from behind the coffee machine. "Lily, thank you so much for coming down." She gave me a hug.

"I'm only too happy to help. So, what do you want? Maybe I can get a few candid shots of you guys making coffee and a few customer interactions?"

She smiled. "Sounds good. Thank you." She glanced around. "It's so busy, so I'd better get back to it."

"Cool. I'll speak to you later."

She rushed to get back to her station. I took the lens cap off my camera and turned it on. I had my trusty Nikon for this. It almost felt like old times when this had been my job. As support—and probably because they wanted more coffee— Will lined up to buy coffee for our group. I wasn't going to say no to another one.

I nudged through the crowd and stood side on to Cory and Amy and took a few shots. I then squeezed behind them— there wasn't much room behind the counter—and took a shot of them from behind, so their heads were fuzzy, but the line came into focus. After that, I wandered around the café and asked people's permission to take photos of them and explained that these would be used on social media. A couple of people said no, but generally everyone was accommodating and said they were only too happy to oblige and how sad it was that Frances was no longer with us.

Busy snapping away, a see-through person took me off guard. *Click. Oh crap.* I lowered the camera. My eyes widened, and I swallowed. *What the hell?* Also, what was he doing here? It was a lot to process.

Fabian Bannister stood at the café entry and tried to see past the customers to the front. Was he here to revel in everyone's sadness, congratulate himself on what he'd done? Was he a serial killer, and this was how he got his jollies? My heart raced. I wanted so badly to tackle him to the ground, smoosh his face into the hard tiles, and handcuff him.

But I couldn't.

I took some deep breaths and looked at Will, who, with Beren, had just received all the coffees. They came over and Will handed me mine. "Here you go." He gave me a funny look. He could probably see that something was wrong. "It's hot in here. Want to take a break?"

"Sounds good."

We went outside, and thankfully, Fabian hadn't noticed me. We stood a few feet from the entry, and I told them what I'd seen. Then I showed them the photo.

"Well, lovie, at least he's not going to be around much longer. Karma?" Imani wasn't wrong.

"Why do you think he dies?" Liv asked.

I shook my head. "I have no idea. Guilt? Maybe they were having an affair? Or maybe someone paid him to kill her, and they're going to get rid of the risk? But why did he show up today?"

"The mind boggles." Will frowned. "Maybe he wanted to see the devastation he's caused? Or maybe he's come to collect his money, because would you really kill someone as a favour?"

Beren sipped his coffee. "Well, whatever the reason, at least he won't be around to do more damage. But then again, if someone paid him to do it, he's a witness. We'd be better off having him alive."

"True." Beren made a good point. "But why is he going to die now?"

"Maybe his next victim is a witch?" Imani cocked her head to the side.

I sucked in a breath. "You're not suggesting me, are you?"

She laughed. "Oh, no, lovie. Sorry. Just in general. Or maybe the next victim is a black belt in martial arts? Or maybe the killer decided they didn't want to pay, and he threatened to tell the police everything?"

Liv's eyes widened, and she stared at me. "He didn't recognise you, did he?"

"No. He didn't even notice me." At least I didn't think so. "I want to see what he does now. We should be watching him." Maybe whatever he did here would give us some clues. I was about to go inside when he and Amy came outside together.

Oh. My. God.

They didn't see us standing to the side against the neighbouring business, but they kept their voices low, so I had no idea what they were talking about. Amy looked angry. She shook her head, and her voice rose. "I don't know what you're doing here, but please leave. Now." Maybe they'd had trouble with him before? Surely she wasn't behind her sister's murder. *Crap.*

We stared at them, Will tensed to intervene if something happened.

"But, Amy, please listen."

"Now's not the time. Goodbye, Fabian." She turned to go inside and noticed us. She grimaced as if to say, I can't deal with this, then continued inside, leaving Fabian standing there, head hanging.

This didn't make sense. He looked upset. Why? And how did they know each other?

Imani, Will, and Beren gave each other looks. I knew what they meant. "Yes, the plot thickens," I said.

Will turned his gaze on me. "So, looks like Frances and Fabian did know each other. Amy knew him too. Maybe your friend was having an affair, and her sister knew."

That didn't gel with what I knew of my friend, but how well did we really know anyone? Sometimes I didn't even recognise myself when I did things like call lightning down to smite people. "I'm so confused right now. Could Amy have wanted her sister dead?"

Will shrugged. "Anything's possible."

Fabian stared at the inside of the shop for a bit, then turned and walked up the hill towards Cronulla Mall. "Should we follow him from now on and see how he dies?"

Imani stared at me, concern clear on her face. "Wow, you're morbid."

"Oh, God, it's not because I want to watch him die, although I won't be sad, but shouldn't we know for sure when he's not a safety issue any more?"

Beren shook his head. "To be honest, this isn't adding up. What if he and Frances weren't a thing? What if he and Frances's sister were a thing? Maybe the sister is next, or maybe the sister got him to kill her. And as I said before, it's better if he's alive, so he can potentially tell the police what happened."

Liv frowned. "What? Why would she have her own sister killed? She's here supporting her sister's business and partner."

I raised a brow. "You don't think she wanted to date Cory, do you? That's not a reason to kill your sister, surely. If it was, there would be many dead women murdered by their siblings, and probably ex-friends murdered by their jealous girlfriend."

"I think it's time we found out what assets Frances really had and who got what when she died." Will was right.

"We should probably follow that idiot as well." Imani

looked up the street to where Fabian had just turned left into the mall.

"I can't leave till I say bye to Amy. Should I feel her out?"

"Subtly, please. If she is involved in her sister's murder, we don't want her twigging that we're suspicious," Beren said.

"Okay."

Imani looked at Will and Beren. "I'll follow him. He doesn't know who I am. You guys stay with Lily."

"I'll go with you." Beren looked at Liv. "Is that okay?"

She smiled. "Of course. Maybe Lily and I can hang around for a while, observe Amy and Cory. See if Amy's flirting with him."

"Good idea, Liv." My friend wasn't just a gorgeous face.

"Okay. Let's do that." Will turned to Beren and Imani. "You two better get a move on before he disappears." Rather than answering, they took off. Will pulled his phone out of his shorts' pocket. "Hey, Phillip. Sorry to bother you on holiday, but we need some info." He listened for a bit, then explained what had happened. "Can you get your friend to pull Frances's financial records, and see if we can get hold of her will?" He nodded. "Yep…. Okay, bye."

Liv and Will came with me when I re-entered the café. I got my camera ready and took some more photos. At least there were no more see-through people. I didn't want to totally block access to my magic because it was bad enough that I couldn't draw from the river. It was like wanting chocolate or cake and not being able to eat it because you were on a diet. The need became greater until you broke down and indulged. Blocking myself from my talent would be the last straw. Besides not wanting a fine, I didn't want to give Bothers the pleasure. *Jerk.*

Liv whispered, "Look at how she's looking at Cory. She's

batting her eyelashes, but he's so down, he hasn't even noticed."

"We men are clueless sometimes," said Will, "but he might've noticed, and he's just not interested. He looks genuinely devastated about Frances."

"He does." That just made me sadder. If her sister did have something to do with it, I wanted her in jail ASAP. My heart kicked up a notch as an idea hit me. "I never saw who was in the white car. What if it wasn't Fabian? What if it was someone else, and that's why there were two cars? What if it was someone Frances knew, and that's why she got into the car?"

Will's eyebrows rose. "You could be right—assuming she didn't know Fabian. Let's go and check."

"Let's. I'll go and say goodbye." I went to the counter and got Amy's attention. "I'm just going for a walk, but text me your email, and I'll send all the shots as soon as I get home. There are some great ones. I've gotten permission from all the customers in those photos, too, so you can use whatever you want."

"Thanks, Lily. You're the best."

"Um, I don't want to pry, but is everything okay?"

She gave me a confused look. "Other than my sister being dead, you mean?" *Ouch.*

"No, sorry. With that guy from before. Is everything okay? He's not a threat or anything, is he?"

Her face relaxed. "Oh, him. No. He's just a guy who's been trying to date me for ages, and he keeps sniffing around. He's harmless. Annoying more than anything. I just have to be firm with him, you know? He's one of those types who can't take no for an answer."

"Well, if he gives you too much trouble, maybe call the police."

She rolled her eyes. "They're useless. They never do anything, and restraining orders don't work either. It's fine. He's harmless and not too bright."

"Oh, okay. Anyway, I'm glad today went well."

She smiled. "Me too."

"Bye, Cory."

He looked up at me as if he'd been in a daze, on automatic pilot making coffees. "Yeah, ah, Lily, isn't it?"

"Yes."

"Thanks for coming today. We really appreciate it."

"Not a problem. If you need anything else while I'm here, let me know."

He gave a nod, then focussed on what he was doing. I turned and joined Will and Liv outside. It was a ten-minute stroll to Frances's place. I looked down at the surf as we walked parallel to the beach, along the top of the Wall. Eventually, we were near where the white car had been. "Can you guys stand just there?" I pointed at where I wanted them. They complied. I lifted my Nikon. "Smile." *Show me the white car Amy was driving the night Frances disappeared.*

My stomach dropped.

There it was, Frances with the door open, bending down to talk to the person inside. The car light hadn't turned on, but it didn't matter. I walked closer and beckoned Will and Liv to move to where I needed them—just to the side of the open door. *Click.* It was still hard to see who was driving, but the person was definitely smaller than Fabian, and my magic wouldn't have shown me the car if it wasn't Amy driving.

Gotcha.

Nausea flipped my stomach. Frances had been betrayed by someone she loved, by family. This was worse than just some random man killing her. But why would Amy do it?

It was time to find out.

CHAPTER 12

That night after cake tasting and dinner, we all sat around and discussed the situation. Beren and Imani hopped on a train and followed him to his stop at Liverpool. They tailed him until he got home; then they came back. "You guys went above and beyond today. How can I pay you back?" They'd spent hours on this, doing something unpleasant when they were supposed to be on holiday.

Beren gave me a kind smile. "It was worth it to know he got home safely. If our summation of the situation is correct, he killed Frances because of Amy. Whether Amy made him or paid him is another thing. But we need him to admit it before he dies. Hopefully he'll be around to admit to it tomorrow."

"Do we think Amy's going to kill him, or do we think he'll kill himself?" Angelica asked. As much as she wasn't going to work while she was here, she still wanted to be in on what was happening.

I shrugged. "We have no idea, but I'm betting Amy kills him. He's a massive loose end." I shuddered thinking about how calm she was today—how calm she'd been since Frances's death. She had no qualms about living with Cory, talking to Frances's friends, pretending to be sad. It was obvious that she felt no guilt. She was a true psychopath.

Will tapped his finger on his thigh. "Maybe Amy was angry with him today because he wasn't supposed to kill Frances? Maybe it was his decision?"

"Even so," Angelica said, "she's an accessory after the fact. Who wouldn't be running to the police with what they knew if it was their sibling? I say she had more than something to do with it."

"Could I just print out one of my pictures of Frances getting into the hire car that night that shows the number plate? Amy must've hired it. I could go to the hire place and check that out with a photo. And when we went to see Cory the first time and she was there, she made out like she'd just gotten there. She wasn't supposed to be in Sydney the night Frances died."

"So she was definitely covering it up." Imani nodded slowly. "I bet she told him to do it. But why did he agree?"

Will rubbed his chin. "Maybe she has something on him, or maybe he loves her, or maybe she offered a lot of money."

I shook my head. "She supposedly has no money. At least, that's what she wants us to believe."

"Unless she was planning on paying him after she got whatever money Frances might leave to her. The other option is that he's scared of her," Liv said. "I mean, if she planned to kill her own sister, she's not exactly someone you want to mess with."

Angelica's poker face was on, but she had her arms folded. "It could be a combination of all three."

I sat up straight. "Oh, God, do you think Cory's in danger?

I mean, if the motive is money, wouldn't Amy end up with the whole café if Cory's out of the way? He might have a will that leaves his share of the café to Frances, but with Frances gone, if he hasn't changed the will, Amy might have a case to have it transferred to her."

Imani's mouth dropped open. "Lily, that's brilliant. She could easily slip him some Valium and do something. It would be easy to tell everyone he was devastated after Frances died, and he couldn't handle it."

I breathed my stress out. "No, actually, I take it back. He wasn't see-through in my pictures today. If she is going to kill him, it won't be in the next few days."

"Doesn't mean she won't kill him eventually if we don't out her to the police," Will said.

The stakes just got a whole lot higher.

I rubbed my forehead. There were so many questions, and we couldn't sit on this forever. "So, what do you think about sending my photo to the police?"

Angelica stared at me. "I think we could, but only as a starting point for any future trial. By the time the police get around to following the lead—going to the hire place, questioning whoever hired the car, looking for more evidence—they're not necessarily going to get the answers we want them to. Besides, there's no time stamp on it. And what if Amy hired the car under an alias? If it is under her name, she could say she picked her sister up to chat and then dropped her off because she wanted to walk her anger off. And then she'll be tipped off that someone knows something. The police won't have the link to the second car, and we can hardly send them a photo of the car going into The Cecil building. That would just be weird. They'd wonder who the stalker taking the photos was and whether they were setting the hire-car driver up."

"Right," said James, "so that's a definite no on sending your photo in, Lily. We don't want to tip this woman off."

Millicent looked at James. "So, are you suggesting Lily needs to catch Amy in the act? What if she doesn't do anything until after we leave?"

I frowned. "My magic usually shows someone see-through not long before they die. I doubt it would show up with more than a week to go. Not that it definitely can't. But my experience has been that it's usually soon."

Imani sipped her tea, then leaned forward and put the cup on the coffee table. Why was it called a coffee table? Why not a tea table, drinks table, or even a water table? I'd have to google it later because it was going to stop me from sleeping tonight. "I think we need someone following Amy and someone following Fabian."

I shook my head. A boulder of guilt dropped into my stomach. "I can't ask you to do that. This is everyone's holiday."

Imani raised a brow. "You're not asking anyone to do anything. We're volunteering, stepping up. It was one thing when your friend died and we thought the police would eventually get around to figuring it out, but now other peoples' lives are at stake, and she might get away with it, I'm not standing by and letting it happen." She looked at everyone in turn. "I know Lily will help me, but if no one else wants to commit, I understand. I can't just sit by and let it happen."

Angelica gave her a satisfied nod. "Yes, dear. I'm with you." She took Phillip's hand and looked him in the eye. "I'm sorry, my love, but I need to help my agents. This doesn't sit well with me either. We'll enjoy our spa visit in the morning, and then I'll give this the afternoon."

He gave her an understanding smile. "That's one of the

main things I love about you—your desire to see justice done. I understand. I'll help too. Whatever you need, my love." He kissed her hand, and her eyes were full of affection. We rarely saw this side of Angelica, and it surprised me every time; it also warmed my heart. Mushy moment over, Angelica donned her poker face and regarded each of us. "So, Lily and Imani are in. Who else wants to help? It's not compulsory, by the way. I won't hold it against anyone who just wants to enjoy their holiday."

Sarah and Lavender gave each other looks of excitement, then shot up their hands. I smiled. Maybe a relaxing holiday wasn't action-packed enough for them. Millicent and James looked at each other. Mum smiled. "If both of you want to help, I'm happy to watch Annabelle. I don't get to do that much back home. I'd love to take her for walks to the beach and just spend time."

Millicent grinned. "I don't want to spend all my time on this case, but I wouldn't mind helping a bit, and maybe James and I can have a bit of an afternoon to ourselves while we're here?"

Mum grinned. "Of course, sweetie! You two deserve some time together too. Consider it taken care of."

Millicent jumped up and hugged Mum. "Thank you. You're an angel."

Beren held Liv's hand. "I'm happy to do a couple of shifts, but I don't want to spend too much time on it because I want to spend time with Liv." Liv couldn't help as much as the rest of us because she wasn't used to being in the field. Also, with her lack of magic, she was a sitting duck for anyone who wanted to hurt her. Not that we were allowed to use magic willy-nilly, but we'd be way more likely to survive if someone attacked us.

Angelica looked at Will. "And… we're waiting on you."

"Oh, of course!" He gave a wry smile. "Sorry. I figured it went without saying that I'd help my gorgeous fiancée with anything she wanted."

"Aw, shucks." I batted my lashes at him.

James pulled a face. "Please don't do that. It's scary."

I stood and went to him, then knelt so we were almost eye to eye. I batted the hell out of my lashes up close and personal. He leaned back as far as possible, but it wasn't enough for him to get away. Imani and Sarah laughed. James flailed his arms. "Get away from me with those creepy eyelashes."

"Children, children, children." Angelica wasn't one to let shenanigans go on too long. "You've had your fun. Now desist, please."

I backed off and stood. I made a siren noise. "Nee-ner, nee-ner, nee-ner. Watch out; the fun police have arrived." I chuckled, and Liv snorted. Everyone else was trying not to laugh… except Angelica. She'd raised an eyebrow and was giving me the stink eye.

If looks could kill, Angelica would've just murdered me. I sat back next to Will and tried not to laugh. "Right, you lot. Let's start working through this." Angelica looked at me, this time without the killing vibes. "Lily, tomorrow morning and then again in the afternoon, I want you at the café to look at Cory through your phone. As soon as he's see-through, I want you to let me know." I nodded. She looked at Beren and then Liv. "You two can take the first shift on Fabian—you'll be safe enough with Beren, dear."

Liv smiled. "I'm happy to be included in the field for a change." She looked at Beren. "And we'll be doing something together."

Beren laughed. "Maybe not quite what I had in mind, but I'll take it."

Angelica turned to my brother. "You and Millicent can hang around here and observe Amy until lunchtime. As soon as one of them's on the move, we'll liaise. I want you to call me straight away."

If only we could've cast tracking spells on their phones. This no-magic business was terrible.

Angelica looked at me and Imani. "You two can take the mid-afternoon to 11:00 p.m. shift on Amy. Sarah and Lavender can take the same shift on Fabian. That way, even if one of them slips our notice, we're still observing one of them. She's not going to get anywhere near him without us knowing about it."

"Good plan," Mum said.

"And because we know he's going to die soon, we shouldn't have to follow both of them for too long."

Liv put her hand up. Ah, it was almost like being back around the conference-room table. "Yes, dear."

"What if she doesn't kill him but he kills himself or he gets hit by a bus?"

Angelica considered the question for a moment. "I'm afraid there's nothing we can do about that. If that happens, we'll lose a chance to out Amy as a killer. It's something we can't control, so let's not think about that now." Angelica cracked her knuckles. *Crick. Crack.* I cringed. "Each team following one of our suspects can take a car. The rest of us can walk or taxi it if we want to get anywhere. Right. Any questions?"

Everyone stayed quiet. Phillip gave a nod. "Right, that's organised. Well done, team. Tomorrow I should have the information on Frances's financials, too, and we can look more closely at Amy's motives. Actually"—he looked at me—"from what you said the other day, your friends are becoming closer with the sister, and you took those photos this morning. Do you think you could be a bit friendlier with Amy, too, try and get to know her more? We could end up with a better picture of her frame of mind and view of her sister."

Hanging out with and being nice to Frances's potential killer wasn't my idea of fun, and it gave me the heebie-jeebies, but I'd do it for Frances. "Yes, I can definitely do that." I looked at Angelica. "Whenever I'm with her, you won't need to have a team on her, so that will save some holiday time." I smiled. I would really owe everyone big time after this. Even though this was their choice, and they offered to help without me asking, I still felt all the guilt for their sacrifice.

Imani shook her head. "Don't worry about that, lovie. Honestly. Let's just get this sorted before your wedding so we can all have a cracking day."

I smiled. "Thanks. You guys are the best friends and family anyone could want."

Lavender grinned at me. "The feeling's mutual." He stood and looked around the room, rubbing his hands together. "Guess what time it is?"

I took one for the team and asked, "What time?"

I should've recognised the twinkle in his eyes. "Cocktail hour!" I had to hand it to him—he knew how to enjoy himself, and he was good at dragging us along with him. And I wasn't complaining. Not one bit.

CHAPTER 13

The next morning, I walked down to Surfer's Brew. I had a clear line of sight to Cory, who was manning the cash register. I held my phone at chest height and pretended I was texting while I looked at him through the camera app. He was solid. Phew. In the interest of supporting him and myself, I went in and bought a cappuccino. It also wouldn't hurt to start trying to be friendly to Amy.

"Morning. It smells delicious in here."

Cory gave me a small smile. "Thanks, Lily. What would you like?" I didn't want to ask him how he was while he was at work—plus, he probably wanted to try and forget for five minutes or at least not focus solely on his loss.

"A cappuccino, thanks, extra chocolate on the top."

Amy, who was barista this morning, laughed. "A woman after my own heart. Coming right up." Argh, I did not have a heart like hers. Hers was black and barely beating. It probably oozed out something disgusting like tar or dog poo.

I went to pay, but Cory shook his head. "No, you can't pay.

It's on the house. You did such great work yesterday. Also, I know you didn't charge, but I want to pay."

I glanced at Amy. She gave me a look that said she pitied him. I turned back to Cory. "Nope. My gift to you guys." I reached across with a five-dollar note.

He put his hand up in a stop gesture. "Definitely not. If you won't charge for your services, I'm not charging for mine."

I smiled. "Okay, fair enough." I glanced at Amy and shrugged. I was the reluctant non-payer for coffee. I moved along to where people picked up the takeaway coffee.

Amy slid my coffee across. "Simone mentioned you're getting married. Are you excited?"

Anger vibrated under my skin, but I pushed through it and smiled. "Super excited." My smile disappeared. "Frances was going to cater it. I can't believe she's gone." My sadness wasn't manufactured, but I was looking for Amy's reaction.

She sniffed. "I know. It's horrific." She sighed and tapped the old coffee grounds out of the thingamajig. "Mum's beside herself. I'm going to go down and get her for the funeral. I don't know exactly when that will be, but hopefully soon."

"I hope it's before I leave. I'd like to say goodbye." Hopefully, the coroner would release the body now that they found Valium and not much else… at least I didn't think they found much else. "Look, if you ever need to talk, I'm here for another week or so. I know Frances would want you and Cory to be looked after." I pretended to come up with an idea. "Hey, do you want to go for a walk this afternoon after you close? We don't have to talk about anything in particular. We can just walk."

She smiled, filled the thingamajig with coffee, and put it back in the machine. "You are so thoughtful. Thank you, Lily. I'm afraid I have to pass." She glanced at Cory, then looked back at me. "Cory's going to his parents' for dinner, and I'm catching up with an old friend, but thanks anyway."

I smiled. "Not a problem." Another customer was standing next to me waiting for their coffee, and another couple was ordering. "I suppose I'd better let you get back to it. You have my number, anyway. If you ever want to chat, let me know."

"Thanks. I will." She smiled again. Argh, I wanted to punch it from her face and scream "how could you?! How could you kill your sister?"

I bade Cory goodbye, too, and left. That poor man. If we didn't solve this in a way that got her arrested, I didn't know how I'd live with myself. Cory—if she didn't decide to kill him herself—was going to be beside himself when he realised he'd let his girlfriend's murderer live in his house and work in their coffee shop. Knowing what Amy stole from Frances and Cory, I was more determined than ever to expose her and solve this.

When I left the café, I went down to the beach, sat on the dry sand, and called James. "Hey. I've just finished there if you and Mill want to start spy duty. I asked if she wanted to go for a walk later this arvo, and she said she was meeting an 'old friend.'"

"Interesting. So she should pretty much be at the café all day?"

"Yep. You guys could sit in the park and watch the cafe from across the road. There isn't a back entrance." Waiting for her to leave was going to be super-duper boring for them.

"We'll be there in fifteen. Do you mind watching out until we get there?"

"Consider it done. Bye." I hung up and stared at the surf for another minute, then retraced my steps back towards the café. I sat on the low concrete wall that bordered the park and the pedestrian area that led to beachside restaurants. Surfer's

Brew was diagonally across the road, under Rydges hotel. I stared at the doorway until my brother, Mum, and Millicent arrived with Annabelle. "Hey, you brought my favourite niece."

James laughed. "Your only niece."

"Okay, my favourite little person in the whole world." I scooped my smiling cutie out of the pram and gave her a big kiss. "You're not making her hang out here all morning, are you?"

Millicent looked at me as if I needed my head examined. "Of course not. Kat has kindly offered to play with her at the beach for a little bit. Then, they're going to walk home."

"Oh, that's nice. She won't get much of a chance to go to the beach back in England, so that's a great idea."

Millicent smiled. "Yep. She loves the sand and when we hold her and run away from the waves." She looked at James. "I think when we get back, we'll make more time for family breaks at the beach. Spain and Portugal have some gorgeous beaches just like here." And with our doorways, it wasn't like they had to travel ages to get there.

"What are you going to do now?" Mum asked.

I was in my jogging gear. "I'm going to go for a run to Wanda and back. After all that cake yesterday, I need to burn some calories, otherwise I won't fit into my dress."

Millicent chuckled. "I remember the pre-wedding stress of fitting into the dress. Try not to worry. How much weight can you put on between now and next weekend?"

"I'm sure if I tried hard enough, it would be a lot." I laughed. "Okay. Have fun. I'll see you guys later." I handed Annabelle to Mum.

Jogging was also good for letting my thoughts wander—not that my thoughts waited for permission. They took themselves for an outing whenever they felt like it. But this was good thinking and processing time. I ran through everything for the wedding and concentrated on my breathing, being careful to keep my pace where I felt uncomfortable, but I could still breathe in through my nose and out through my mouth. They'd done studies that proved that more oxygen reached active tissue when breathing through your nose because of nitric oxide, which is only produced by your nose. It helps your blood vessels relax and widen.

Ah, the useless information I carried in my brain. No wonder my memory was terrible—my head had an overload of random crap to sift through to find anything.

Today was a pleasant twenty-three degrees, but by the time I ran to Wanda and back home, I was a sweaty mess. I showered, dressed, and found Will and Imani downstairs playing chess. "Wow, Angelica thought of everything when she outfitted this house."

Imani frowned at me. "Yes, well, maybe she could've left the chess set out."

Will chuckled. "You didn't have to play."

The board had way more black pieces than white. Will was winning. "I didn't know you were a poopy loser."

Imani scowled at me. "I'm not a poopy loser. I just don't like to lose. Does anyone?"

"Fair point." I held up my phone. "I'll be ready to film the tantrum when the inevitable happens." I waggled my brows. Imani gave me a death stare. I took a photo and laughed.

"Stop distracting her, Lily. I want to finish the game." He only wanted to finish because he was going to win.

"Anyone want a water, tea, or coffee?" Imani wanted tea and Will a coffee. I busied myself in the kitchen and brought our drinks out. I was just having water because running was thirsty business.

My phone rang. Angelica's name came up on the screen. "Hello. Is everything okay?"

"Yes, dear. Why would you think it wasn't?"

"Um, you don't usually ring for no reason, and with everything that's been going on, I just assumed there was a problem."

"Quite the opposite, actually. We have the information on the financials for the café and Frances. The café was doing quite well. The after-tax profit for last financial year was a hundred and seventy thousand dollars. And that was before the boyfriend came on board."

"So that was her income?"

"Yes. And Cory isn't working in the business full-time either. He has a well-paying job on contract to a large bank. He works in online security. Which is probably how they can afford that expensive apartment you were telling me about. They bought it—it's not rented."

My mouth dropped open. "They really had some cash, then. Wow."

"Well, dear, it appears as though Cory and Frances each owned less expensive apartments, which they sold to buy this one, so they had equity, but still… they weren't short of a quid."

"If they own the unit together, Amy would have to sell it to get her share if something happened to Cory. She's not going to inherit the whole thing."

Angelica tut-tutted. "Yes, but she still stands to inherit the café and a reasonable sum of money. She was named as the main beneficiary in the will, and Cory isn't a half-owner of the café. They had it structured so there was a seventy/thirty split.

Frances was the majority owner. Frances left fifty thousand dollars to her mother and the rest to Amy."

"Oh, wow. Okay. So, Amy has good motive."

"Yes, dear. The only link we don't have is why she roped Fabian into it."

"She claimed he wanted to date her and won't leave her alone." Hmm…. "Maybe she's stringing him along?"

Angelica didn't answer for a bit. "I don't know, dear. Would you kill someone just to get someone's romantic interest? It's more likely that they're already involved, and she's manipulated him.

"She mentioned that he wasn't very bright. Maybe she used him to kill Frances so there would be no physical evidence linking her to it. Also, the way he killed her… there's no way Amy would've been able to practically carry Frances all that way to the water, swim her to the edge of the ocean pool, lift her, and throw her over." Amy was a couple of inches shorter than Frances, and I hadn't seen her exercising at all. It really would've been hard for her to do what Fabian had done.

"That makes sense, but we have to prove it."

"Yes, we do. One thing at a time, I suppose. Besides, if we catch her in the act, the police can figure the rest out." I really hoped she would make it easy for us.

"I have to go now, dear. Speak to you later."

"Bye." As I put my phone on the table, Imani's shoulders drooped.

"I'm never playing this stupid game again."

Will smirked. "That's too bad. I like winning."

She pressed her lips together. "So help me, if I had my magic, you'd have an itchy bum right now."

I laughed. "Remind me never to challenge you to something I'm good at." I versed Will, and it was close, but he beat me. After that, we hung out, had lunch, relaxed, and then it was time for Imani and me to do our shift watching Amy. We took the car, and I drove. I parked outside Dunningham Park, where I'd left James and Millicent earlier, and I high-fived them. James gave me a "why did you do that" look. "It's the official handover sign. You're free to go. Did anything happen?"

James said, "No. She went up the street for a break for twenty minutes, but it was for a vape."

"Oh, she's a murderer *and* a health nut. Interesting." From what I'd read in the news, vaping could be just as deadly and damaging as smoking. At least vapers smelled better. I liked to see the positive as much as I could.

"So, you guys are ready to roll?" Millicent asked.

"Yep, lovies. Have a nice afternoon together."

"Will do." James smiled. "I'm going to show Mill a few of the places I used to hang out as a teen."

Millicent grabbed his hand. "It's nice to finally see where you're from. Cronulla is a gorgeous place. I definitely want to come back one day."

After saying goodbye, Millicent and James left at a leisurely pace. Happiness infused my chest with warmth. It really filled my heart to see them enjoying time together. This was what we'd strived so hard for over the last year—a chance to live a normal life outside of work. And I still had to pinch myself, but we'd managed it.

"What are you grinning about?" Imani's head tilted to the side as she peered at me.

"Just enjoying that we have a life, and we're free. It feels good."

She nodded. "It feels damn good."

We settled in for the afternoon. Luckily, Imani was interesting to chat to because otherwise, I would've died of boredom, sitting in the same spot with nothing else to do. The café closed at five. I took a photo of Cory as he was leaving. Still solid. Relief filtered through me. One less thing to worry about tonight.

Cory and Amy went back to the apartment together. Imani and I sat in the car a few doors down, so she wouldn't notice us if she left, which she was supposed to do. I'd also looked around for Agent Bothers, but I hadn't spied him. Maybe he was going to pop out of a doorway any moment and come find me. *Please, God, no.* I hadn't seen him all day. Either he was getting better at hiding, or Angelica had made that phone call.

Even though she'd told me she couldn't go for a walk because she was going out, she didn't emerge until six forty. She hopped into a blue mini. I sucked in a breath. "That's Frances's car. See the number plate."

FRANXO. Even her number plate was sweet. It was as if she were giving a kiss and cuddle to anyone reading the plate. Now her evil sister was driving her car.

"She's a disgusting human. The sooner we put her away, the better." Imani's voice held anger. I loved it when she went into werewolf mode. Okay, so there were no such things as werewolves, but if there were, Imani would totally be one. I expected her to bust out the claws and growl any moment.

Amy pulled out. We were on the move. I followed at a safe distance. We drove for twenty minutes, ending up at a bay-side suburb called Brighton-Le-Sands. It was difficult to get parking, so I dropped Imani close to where Amy had parked, and I drove another block before I found a spot. This was getting tricky. We should've worn some kind of disguise. We'd have to take extra care to stay far from her so we weren't recognised. Unfortunately, that meant no listening in on any conversations.

I got out and texted Imani. She called me. "She's met Fabian outside a Greek restaurant. They've gone inside." She hung up and texted me the address.

Crap. At least we knew where they were, but now we'd have to wait for them to eat, and we couldn't even walk around and see anything. I so wanted my magic so we could listen in. When I reached the street with the restaurant, I smiled. "Sarah, Lav!" I gave them both a hug. "I forgot you'd be here." Since they were following Fabian, it stood to reason.

"Why don't I go and grab us some takeaway," Imani said. "What's everyone in the mood for?"

I pointed to a Turkish place that was open to the street and mainly did takeaway. "They have good food. I'm in the mood for a kebab. They have great gozleme too." I dragged a breath through my nose. "Mmm, I can smell it."

"So, which is it?" Imani put one hand on her hip. "Or are you getting both?"

"Hmm, that's not a bad idea. I'll get one beef kebab and one cheese and feta gozleme, and I'm happy to share them too. Does anyone want to go halves?"

Lavender smiled. "That sounds like a great idea. I'm in." He high-fived me. "I'll pay."

"No, I'll pay." I owed my friends at least a dinner for everything they were doing.

"No, I'll pay," said Imani. "I offered to get the food. Besides, Will paid for the hire cars, and we're staying at your house for free. We've been eating your food."

I rolled my eyes. "But you're a guest in our country. It's only polite for us to do all that."

"Don't be ridiculous." She looked at Sarah. "What would you like?" Sarah settled on a chicken kebab. "I'll be back soon."

Well, at least this night wasn't a total bust. We were on a main road, and a noisy Harley drove by. Plenty of people were walking past as well, and we had to move out of the way. We ended up squished against a shop wall. "This place is happening." Lavender looked around.

"It's always been busy. So many people come here on the weekend, plus there's lots of apartments around here, and people like to go to a beach without surf. There aren't many in Sydney. Mainly here and on Sydney Harbour."

Sarah gazed across the road at the tall pine trees and water. "You guys have so much outdoors stuff to do. It's so laid back. I could live here." She sighed.

I shook my head. "You're not allowed to move here now that I'm living in England. No way, woman. Will wouldn't be impressed either."

She patted my shoulder. "It's okay, Lily. I'm not planning on moving any time soon. I'd miss you all too much. And I love my job and working with this one." She threw her arm around Lavender, and he slid his arm around her waist. They would've made such a good couple if he wasn't gay. Would either of them find someone soon? They didn't strike me as lonely, and neither of them said much about wanting a partner. Maybe they were both happy by themselves? They did a lot together, so maybe that was enough for now.

Imani returned with our food in less than ten minutes. We found a bench across the road and ate. After that, we took turns watching the restaurant door. After two hours, I was ready for bed. "Would it look weird if I lay down here and had a nap?"

Sarah looked around. "Yes. Definitely. Maybe if you had a picnic blanket, it wouldn't look so weird, but without one, you'll look you've been on the pop."

I looked at her, horrified. "I would not. My clothes are fine, and my hair is brushed. I'm hardly vomiting. You're way too harsh."

She laughed. "I was just joking. I love to get you all riled up."

"Saved by the appearance of our marks." Imani was watching the door across the road.

I gave Sarah and Lavender a hug. "See you guys later. Have fun."

"You too." Sarah waved and followed Lavender down the street to where I assumed their car was.

"How are we going to see where she's going and get to the car at the same time?" Amy's car was in a different street to mine, but if Imani had to wait here, I'd have to drive around the block to pick her up, and then Amy would be gone.

"Run back to your car and come around. I'll stand where Amy's car is now. You can pick me up." That was a bad idea since it was a main road, but I didn't have a better one. "Okay, cross the road with me, then I'm hoofing it."

As soon as the walk light turned green, I sprinted. At least Amy was still sucking face with Fabian. So, they were dating. Was it all so she could manipulate him, or did she actually like him? Her claim that he wouldn't leave her alone and that she kept telling him to go away appeared to be a lie—she wasn't running from him tonight. Not to mention, she'd said to me she was meeting "an old friend" when she turned me down for a walk. *Interesting.* I figured she'd fed me a story, but you never knew.

I hopped in the rental car and drove as fast as I dared around the block. It took a bit before I could turn left onto the main road, but finally, I managed. Amy's car was leaving as I got there. I put my blinker on and pulled next to her newly vacated spot. Imani jumped in. "They're both in her car."

"Did he drive here?"

She shrugged. "I'll call Sarah. Lavender's driving."

Imani made the call. After a few back and forths, she hung up. "He did drive here."

"So he thinks they'll be back later to get his car, I bet."

"But she's planning on killing him. Is that what you think?"

I glanced at her. "Yep. Unless they have an unintended car crash. Or maybe it's an intended car crash? Or maybe she'll make him get out of the car for something and run him over?"

"She used him to kill her sister. What would make her do the actual killing this time, and why now?" Imani had a good point.

"Maybe she's worried he'll blab? Also, maybe it's easier for her to kill him because he's not family. She didn't grow up with him. Who knows?" Whatever was going to happen, he was see-through in my camera, so something was going to occur soon.

The sun had long since set. We were headed back to the Shire, but instead of turning off towards Cronulla, Amy kept driving straight. We ended up on the main road that travelled south, away from Sydney. "Where do you think she's going?" Imani watched the car a few spots in front.

"I don't know. This is the way back to Nowra, where she lives, but that's over two hours away. She might be planning on going into the national park."

"There'd be plenty of opportunity to kill him with no one watching, I would imagine."

"You would imagine correctly." The weather was warming up, so people might be camping in some places, but the national park covered a massive area, and there'd be sure to be somewhere they could be alone.

Imani's phone rang. She put it on speaker. It was Sarah. "Hey, guys. We're two cars behind you. Where do you think they're going?"

We were approaching a set of lights with a left turn-off. I was sure now. "The national park." Thankfully, two of the five cars between us veered left, too, so we didn't look so obvious following her. This was also the way to the townships of Maianbar and Bundeena—suburbs on the Port Hacking River. Instead of driving all the way around, you could catch the ferry there from Cronulla. But there were many turnoffs to isolated beaches, bushwalks, and campgrounds on the road as well.

We passed the unmanned ticket office—anyone visiting the national park needed to buy a day ticket or season pass. If you were going through to one of the two towns, you didn't need to buy one. We wouldn't be here long, and I doubted the national park officers were policing anything at ten o'clock at night. The one-lane-each-way windy road was scarier in the dark, but Amy was a slow driver, so it wasn't too hairy.

Tall gum trees grew close to the road, blocking the moon-light. One wrong move and it would be easy to slide straight into a deadly trunk. There was also a lot of thick scrub. If she managed to kill him out here somewhere, the body might go undiscovered for weeks, if not months. "How had she conned Fabian into coming all the way out here?" I was thinking aloud, and I hadn't realised I'd said anything until Imani answered.

"Maybe she didn't con him. She might have just suggested they go for a drive and get romantic? He is into her, if you didn't notice."

"True." I bit my bottom lip. "It's super sus coming all the way out here, though. Surely there are places to canoodle that are closer to home. It makes me think she's definitely planning something untoward."

Imani said, "Well, if she is, we'll be here to stop her. I don't like Fabian, but if she kills him, there's one less witness—probably the only witness—who knows her involvement in Frances's murder. We need him alive."

"Well, if we can pin his murder on her, and the police see Valium was used in both cases, surely they'll consider her involvement in her sister's murder. Failing that, at least she'll go away for one killing."

"True." Letting someone get killed with less than a week to go until my wedding didn't sit right with me. It felt like bad karma, even though the guy was a murderer. I'd rather he spent his life in jail. Besides, Cory would want answers. Maybe Fabian would provide them to rat out Amy when faced with the fact that she tried to kill him. Yes, none of that had happened yet, and we still hadn't proven she was behind her sister's murder, but I had to rationalise this somehow, and that's what I was going with until I knew differently. Besides, she'd driven her sister to The Cecil and let her leave pretty much straight away with Fabian. I couldn't see how she wasn't involved somehow.

"She's turning off."

I put my blinker on. I didn't want to tip her off, but we were two cars behind, and Lavender needed warning. As soon as we rounded the corner, I slowed and pulled over to the side. "Can you call Sarah on speaker, please?"

Imani did as I asked. "Hi, Sarah. Lily wants to tell you guys something. Can you put it on speaker?"

"Done."

"Hey, guys. Just pull over behind me for a sec. I don't want to be too close behind her. She'll notice us. According to my maps, there isn't a turn-off for a while, so we won't lose her."

"How long will you wait?"

That was the sixty-four-million-dollar question. "It's a balance between giving her enough time to not kill him but giving her enough time that it's clear that's what she's doing."

Imani looked at me, her expression mildly shocked. "That's a bit of a risk. And what if they're out here to get it on? That will be awkward." She smirked.

I rolled my eyes. "Very funny. Let's just assume the worst. What do you suggest?"

She thought about it. "Fine. I don't have any better ideas. Have we waited long enough?"

"Give it another minute."

Another car came around the corner and passed us. "They might get there first." Lavender's voice came through the phone.

"They might. I hope they don't spoil anything. Unless she has backup?"

"That's something we haven't considered," said Sarah.

"Okay, love. Time to get going." We all said goodbye, and Imani hung up. Then I took her advice and drove.

The car in front of us travelled just under the speed limit. I tried not to get antsy, but then again, Amy hadn't been driving fast either. Our timing was going to be okay... I hoped. If only we could've tracked her car with a spell. I could imagine applying for that through the alphabet-soup division.

Imani stared out of the windscreen. "That car looks familiar."

"It's so dark, how can you even tell?"

"It's a skill from years of agenting. Now if I can remember

where I last saw it." Her brow furrowed, and after a minute, she slapped her thigh, and I jumped.

"Jesus, don't scare the driver."

She grinned. "Sorry. I don't want you to put us into a tree."

"Yeah, neither do I."

"Anyway, do you want to know whose car it is?" She watched me expectantly.

"Do tell. I can't wait." I could wait because I had a suspicion of who it might be. The only person who might be following—unless it was an accomplice of Amy's—was my worst annoying nightmare.

"Agent Bothers."

"Nooooooo! I was hoping you weren't going to say that. Well, he's in front of us, and he has no idea why we're here, so maybe he'll just keep driving and not arrive until we have the situation in hand?" As if we didn't have enough to worry about.

"I'll cross my fingers for us." Ha, if only that was as good as casting a spell.

"By the way, how do you think he always knows where I am?" I'd figured before that he'd always just followed me from home, but I was starting to think I'd been wrong about it.

She looked at me and narrowed her eyes. "We haven't been drawing magic, and we haven't been checking our devices for magical bugs. Maybe he did something to the cars when we were asleep?"

But in order to see if there was a spell, we had to draw magic, which we weren't allowed to do. That was ridiculous. "Is that even legal? We haven't done anything wrong. This surveillance is out of hand. It's not like we're criminals. We're law enforcement, for squirrel's sake." Oh, how I missed my squirrels. They could cheer me up like nobody's business, and they'd help take Bothers down without me getting into trouble. Can't charge a squirrel for biting. If I'd had more time, I would've trained some possums or maybe cockatoos. Those birds were destructive little critters when they wanted to be. A flock of those would be the perfect havoc creators. Or maybe an army of huntsman spiders? I shuddered. That might be a creature too far, even for me.

There was a sign for a car park up ahead. I cut my lights, which made it hard to see, but I didn't want our approach to be noticeable. Lavender, quick man that he was, turned his lights off too. I slowed right down. Finally, we reached a short road, which opened into a small car park. And wouldn't you know it, there was a car, and it wasn't Bothers.

I parked, blocking Amy's car in, and cut the engine. *Please can we be here at the right time.*

Lavender parked next to me. We all jumped out, and I resisted the urge to draw my magic and make a return to sender and a shield. I felt naked as I approached the car. It was hard to see through the window but not impossible. There didn't seem to be anyone in there. I opened the driver's door and peered inside. "Gone."

Imani gave a nod and started on the sandy path between the trees. We followed quietly. She stopped after a minute to listen. There were voices a little way ahead. My heart beat faster, and my breathing rate increased. I shouldn't be scared because there were four of us and two of them, and when it came down to it, we had magic, and they didn't.

My eyes widened. What if one of us killed him because he attacked us? Oh, God, I hadn't considered that. Was it our fault he was going to die? Had we got it all wrong and this really was just a romantic venture into the national park? I couldn't deal with those thoughts right now. I took a deep breath and concentrated on listening. At the very least, we had to confirm what was going on and wait for them to finish.

He was going to die, and we needed to know why.

The sound of a car pulling into the car park reached us. Argh, Bothers was coming. I didn't need that distraction. I glanced behind. The cars weren't visible this far along the path. Hopefully he'd be quiet and try and sneak up on us—I didn't want him tipping off our quarry. I almost ran back to tell him to shush but decided against it when Imani started walking again.

As we snuck closer, Amy's voice was clearer above the sound of crickets and a couple of frogs. "I just don't love you enough to keep you." I ripped my phone out of my pocket and pressed Record on video. I wanted to get all of this. I held it up, hoping it would pick up everything. "Poor, poor Fabian. You thought if you killed my sister for me that I'd profess my undying love for you. You're so naïve and desperate. At least I bought you dinner on our last night together. Don't say I never gave you anything." She laughed. *Yikes.*

Fabian mumbled something that sounded like. "Please don't. You wanted my help, and I gave it to you. You promised we'd be together forever if I killed her." His words were slurred. Had she used drugs on him too?

I couldn't see past Imani's creeping form. How was Amy going to kill him? Maybe we should hurry up. Also, I was kind of relieved it wasn't our fault he was going to die. Hopefully we could stop it.

"Well, I couldn't do it myself—I'm not a strong swimmer, and killing her any other way would have left too much evidence. Of course you wouldn't understand. Idiot. Anyway, promising you my undying love was necessary. And now, I don't want any loose ends. I deserve the life that's coming to me. Frances was uppity, always rubbing it in how much better she was and how well she was doing. And who was looking after Mum and working a dead-end job in a supermarket? I had to take matters into my own hands, and, well, she got what she deserved, and so did I. I might even keep Cory around until I get sick of him. Frances said he's good in bed." Her laugh was more like a cackle this time.

Was there a specific laugh people undertaking evil used in the murderous moment? Certainly sounded like it. And at least I had her motive recorded and her confession. We had everything we needed.

I tapped Imani on the shoulder and showed her my phone. She nodded, understanding that it had gotten all of it. I mouthed, "Now?" She nodded again.

It was go time. I turned and gestured to Sarah and Lavender.

I kept my phone recording and held it in front of me—not that we could see anything in the dark. A small light was ahead, but nothing bright.

The faint glow appeared to be from a phone. Fabian was lying on the ground, his arms tied behind his back. Amy held something shiny in her hand. A large kitchen knife. My mouth dropped open as she placed it at his throat. Imani shouted, "Drop it!"

Amy's eyes bugged open. Once she assessed the situation, she grinned manically. "Get in line." She pushed the knife into his throat.

I didn't think.

The portal to the river opened within me, and I called to my magic. A lightning bolt speared from the sky and hit the knife. Sparks glittered in the darkness, falling harmlessly to the sandy ground. Amy snatched her hand back and shook it. A trickle of blood leaked from a small cut to Fabian's throat. We'd gotten here in time, and I'd managed not to smite her in a panic.

Amy eyed the knife and dove for it. Imani tackled her. Since I'd already drawn my magic, I might as well keep going. The fines were going to rack up. I placed a freeze spell on Amy.

"Cease and desist, Lily Bianchi. You're under arrest. Cut off your access to the power, and put your hands above your head."

What. The. Hell? He had to be joking.

Sarah gasped, and Lavender spun around to stare at Agent Bothers. Imani had managed to place Amy in a better hold because of my freeze spell, which was good because now I'd dropped my magic, the spell fizzled out, and Amy was writhing under her, trying to escape.

I slid my phone into my back pocket—still recording—and put my hands on my head. Other than that, I ignored the two useless agents and turned to Lavender and Sarah. "Do you guys think you could call the police? If you can't get service, just put Fabian and Amy in the car, and once you're out of the national park, it should be okay. You could also drop them to Sutherland Police Station—it's the biggest station in the Sutherland Shire and much closer than Miranda or Cronulla. Use the GPS."

Before Lavender could answer, Bothers—who had a gun pointed at me—pushed past them. "Turn around, Miss Bianchi." His little helper slapped magic-blocking cuffs on me.

Sarah planted her hands on her hips. "You've got to be joking. She just caught a killer."

Bothers looked Sarah up and down and sneered. "Maybe stick to modelling, honey, and we'll stick to law enforcement."

Sarah's eyes widened, and she balled her fists. I gave a small head shake. "Let it go. He's an idiot. We'll fix this. It's fine."

"But you can't go to jail. You're getting married in a few days. What about your hen's night?"

"It'll be fine. Just help Imani."

Lavender gave a chin tip towards Amy and Fabian. "Don't worry, Lily. We'll get them sorted." He grabbed my arm. "I'll also call Angelica and tell her the situation."

"Please do."

"If you're finished, it's time to go. Straight to prison." Bothers laughed, and it sounded too much like Amy's psychotic giggle. His sidekick stood next to me, an evil smile on her face and a ball of light floating above her hand. What was wrong with these people?

Sarah gave me a quick hug as she passed. When she let me go, I stared at the smarmy agent. "Aren't you even interested in what we're doing here?" I couldn't believe he hadn't asked any questions.

"Nope. All I know is that I finally caught you in the act. I knew you'd break the law when I first met you. You have the look of a troublemaker." He shoved me towards the cars. "Now get walking, or we'll add resisting arrest to the charges."

"You are such a moron. I just solved a murder and helped catch the murderer whilst stopping another murder. You can't tell me that it wasn't a good reason to use magic."

"Not only did you do all that, you cast a spell on a non-witch. Both those non-witches will have to be mind wiped. Do you realise how much trouble you've caused?" He opened the back door of their car and shoved me down and in. So rude. I could've done it without his help.

"I said it before, and I'll say it again—you're a moron of the highest order, Agent Bothers."

He slammed the door on me without comment, but not before I saw the scowl on his face. I'd gotten to him. *Ha!* It was the tiniest of victories, but I'd take it.

I sat back in the seat, my arms uncomfortable, pinned behind me. Well, this was great. I was supposed to be preparing for my wedding, but now I was headed to lock-up. Will wasn't going to be happy, and Mum was going to have a conniption. But I couldn't let that get to me because I'd do the same thing again.

Frances was finally going to get justice.

CHAPTER 14

They'd taken me to a holding cell in the city specifically for witches. They were charging me for unauthorised magic use, magic use in front of a non-witch, two counts of magic use against a non-witch, and using magic to deprive a non-witch of liberty.

You had got to be kidding me.

I sat at a table in an interview room, my hands in front of me in magic-blocking cuffs. Thankfully, I was with my new lawyer, Robyn, and Angelica and Will. Nausea bubbled up my throat. Surely I hadn't just heard Robyn correctly. "How many years?!" My voice was a bit on the loud side because I wasn't dealing with this well. I thought I'd be fine, but if I was found guilty, I wouldn't be out of here until my ovaries were practically dried up and my hair was going grey. As much as I didn't want kids now, I didn't want that final decision to be taken from me. Not to mention, being locked up wasn't going to be a picnic. What sort of witches was I going to have to try and get along with? And no squirrels, no cappuccinos, and no double-chocolate muffins. No Will cuddles, no Abby and Ted. My eyes burned with tears. This was just too depressing for words.

Robyn, a forty-something woman with shiny, straight brown hair, perfect make-up, and an eye for gorgeous shoes, managed to also have a voice laced with confidence, which made me feel better, even if the words were horrific. "The sentence carries a term of ten to twenty-five years."

Fear flared on Will's face before he shut it down. So much for being out before my wedding. Will would find someone else and have three high-school-aged kids by then. I put my hands over my face because I didn't want anyone to see me cry. What if bloody Bothers was watching on a camera somewhere. *Stuff him.* I sniffled and wiped my eyes, then sat up straight. "We're going to fight it, right?" I couldn't give up, not on day one anyway.

Robyn smiled, reminding me of a lion. "Of course, Lily. You acted to save a life and to solve a murder. There's no judge that I know of who will say you used magic unreasonably under the circumstances. I'm working on getting the charges dismissed, but there's due process, and I have to write my presentation to the judge. They're refusing bail, so you'll be in here for at least two days. These circumstances are highly unusual—they're being unreasonably tough on you. I've never seen anything like it."

"Agent Bothers—"

"Isn't it Brothers?" Robyn asked.

"Yes, but I call him Bothers because he keeps bothering us." She smirked. "He's had it in for me since we got here. That bit's on my phone too. I recorded everything."

Robyn gave me an "Oh?" look. "I haven't seen that yet. We only just retrieved your belongings from the police." She took a small plastic bag out of her briefcase. It had my wallet and phone in it.

Angelica pressed her lips together. "They better not have tampered with anything. If they push this too hard, I'm going to take it up with my contacts back home. Agent *Bothers* is going to regret the day he crossed swords with us."

"I never took the spell off my phone. It's protected." I'd done one of those spells that you tied off, so I didn't have to be holding magic to use it, and it only used a tiny bit of my own power to maintain. After everything that happened with the directors, I never wanted to leave myself open to anyone spying on my conversations. I might have also forgotten to take it off in the excitement of coming over here.

Yay for my bad memory.

"Good work, dear." Angelica smiled. "I knew I'd make a good agent out of you one day."

I chuckled. "Feel free to take all the credit. I don't mind."

Will laughed.

The door opened, and Bothers stood there. He glowered at everyone and finished on me. "Time's up. Prisoner has to go back to the cell."

Angelica looked at her watch, then stood and gave him a classic Angelica stare down. "We have thirty minutes with Miss Bianchi. It's only been fifteen. I suggest you back out of here and shut the door if you don't want an international incident." She approached him and stood in his personal space. "I'm head of the English PIB, which I'm sure you already know, and I'm done messing around, little man. When I'm finished with you, you'll be lucky to get a job at MacDonald's."

Ooh, she went for the jugular. I loved that woman.

He opened his mouth to speak, but nothing came out. He stammered for a bit before he managed to wrangle control of his mouth. He turned and looked up at the clock above the door. "You've only got thirteen minutes. I'll be back then." He stuck his nose in the air and left, slamming the door behind him.

Angelica's smile was serene as she sat. "Now, let's look at that video."

I unlocked the phone, brought up the video, and pressed Play, then set it in the middle of the table. Will was sitting next to me, and he leaned over and took my hand while he looked across at the phone on the table.

The video from last night played. It was pretty dark, but we could still see a bit, thanks to the iPhone nighttime tech. It was brighter than I could've hoped for. Everyone sat riveted through it, and Angelica looked proud when I used my magic. When Bothers came onto the scene, Will growled. After hearing our exchange, Will said, "Yes, Lily, he's a moron. A massive one."

My phone even recorded the car trip here, where he joked with his partner about taking me down and how he'll get a promotion for it. I rolled my eyes. Eventually, we'd listened to thirteen minutes, and Robyn shut it off. "I'll finish watching this later before I do my brief. Tweedledum will be back any second now."

The door opened just as she finished speaking. Will leaned over and gave me a kiss on the lips. "Don't worry, my love. We'll get you out of here ASAP." He touched my face and looked at me as if his heart was breaking.

I gave him a sad smile. "It's okay. I'll be fine. I'm in a cell by myself. Plenty of time to get my beauty sleep before the wedding." *Please, can I get out of here before then?* I tried not to let my worry show on my face. Will was already upset and scared for me. If I showed strength, it would be easier on everyone else.

He smiled. "I love you, Lily."

"I love you too."

Angelica and the lawyer were playing defence, standing between the frothing Bothers and me and Will. Will gave me one last kiss, then stood slowly. He watched me as he walked backwards to the door. I stood and waved both hands since I was in cuffs. Oh dear, how sad. I couldn't help giggling—okay, it was partly caused by nerves. This was ridiculous, but I trusted my people to get me out of here. Angelica and Will had never ever let me down. I just hoped they managed to get me out of here before the wedding. I wasn't against marrying in England, but that wasn't the point. I hadn't done anything wrong, and Mum had done so much work to organise this. Plus, it wouldn't be quite the same without the sparkling waters of Sydney Harbour behind us when we said "I do."

And worst of all, I didn't want Bothers to win. His smarmy smirk was well in place when I reached him, and there was a cruel glint in his eyes. "Don't plan on making your wedding. You'll be an old lady by the time you get out of here."

I shook my head. "What's wrong with you? You're a psychopath. Don't they do psych evaluations for this job, or maybe even IQ tests? You really shouldn't be in law enforcement." This guy was a menace to good witches everywhere.

He pushed me out of the room and shut the door. "Nothing's wrong with me. I just enjoy cutting down uppity witches who think they're above the law. Now, stop talking, or you'll regret it."

"What are you going to do, keep waffling at me?"

An electric shock zapped my arm, and I stifled a shout. What. The. Hell.

"Or I'll do that." He smiled.

"You are so going down, Bothers. Just you wait. You have no idea who you're dealing with." The cranky look on his face was worth the next zap, and since it didn't take me by surprise, it wasn't so bad. Kind of like a needle when it first punctures the skin. I'd been through much worse in my life.

Bring it, Brothers. Just bring it.

CHAPTER 15

As it turned out, I was stuck in the cell for three days before they came and got me to appear before the judge. The evidence had to be gone over by both sides, and they would've had to get statements from my friends. They'd taken my statement the night they arrested me. Thankfully, it hadn't been Bothers. I had no doubt he'd change what I said to make me look more guilty. Not that I hadn't done what they were accusing me of… which was what worried me. How much leeway would they give? Were all the witches connected with law enforcement here bullies and magic haters?

I was about to find out.

The door opened, and two female guards stood there. One came in and cuffed my hands in front of me. The other held the door and shut it after we exited. My hands sweated, and I yawned. I'd maybe had two-hours sleep last night. The bed was uncomfortable, and I hadn't known when this hearing would be. Not to mention everything that went through my head about being locked up for more than ten years.

Dizziness engulfed me, and I swallowed the vomit back down. One of the guards looked at me, concern on her face. I probably looked unwell, and I doubted she wanted me to throw up on her.

Gah, I needed to focus on something else, anything, and save my panic attack for when I knew what was happening. *Squirrels, think of squirrels.* An image of GTB popped into my head, but it only made me feel worse. I blinked tears back. Squirrels didn't have long lives. If I was found guilty, I'd never see my squirrel buddies again. I hated myself for it, but I couldn't stop the tears. My cheeks were wet by the time I was handed over to Robyn and one of her associates, a young man with neat, side-parted brown hair and silver-framed glasses. He was good-looking in a nerdy way, and he gave me a sympathetic look.

Robyn dug into her bag and brought out a tissue. "It's a bit early for the waterworks. Just wait till after this hearing before you decide your life is over. We've got you. This is Horace, and he'll be assisting me today."

I sniffled and wiped my eyes and cheeks, then blew my nose. "Hi, Horace. Nice to meet you. Sorry for… this." I gestured to my face. "It's a bit overwhelming." It might've also brought back feelings from when I'd first gone to England to help find James, and they threw me in a cell. I was way more naïve back then, and whilst I'd been worried, I'd been confident they'd release me. This time, I had no idea how unreasonable and inflexible they'd be, based on Bothers' behaviour.

He gave me a kind smile. "Robyn's the best there is. Try not to worry." He didn't exactly say they had this in the bag, but he probably didn't want to give me false hope. No one knew what the outcome would be until we sat in front of the judge. Would they take this to trial? And all this because of one jealous psychopath. How Frances managed to come from the same womb as her sisterly monstrosity was beyond me.

And how was all that going? Were Amy and Fabian in jail, or had they let them go? Had all this been for nothing? Surely they couldn't let Amy go at least—we'd caught her red-handed. But she would likely throw him under the bus. The police would want to know why she was trying to kill him, and he'd hopefully said something. Knowing Amy, she might've said he killed her sister, and he wanted to kill her, too, so she was defending herself. Hmm, maybe I was catastrophising because I was already stressed. I should've asked Angelica when she came in the first time, but I'd been too preoccupied with the potential prison sentence.

"Lily?" Robyn was staring at me.

"Oh, sorry. Did you say something?"

She smiled. "It's time to go."

I walked with them and my guards down a couple of long corridors, the fluorescent lighting casting a sallow sheen on everyone's skin. We went through a security door and into a foyer with two lifts. We got in one and went up two floors, then through a security checkpoint and metal detector before coming to another larger high-ceilinged foyer with six doors leading off it. We entered one of the doors, a security guard granting us entry.

The courtroom looked like any other one I'd ever seen on TV. I'd never been inside one before. Seats fanned out from a central aisle, which we walked down. Robyn led us to the front row left, and we sat, me in the middle of my defenders.

Unfortunately, none of my friends and family were here. Probably because they were witnesses in this matter, or maybe because the alphabet-soup brigade were trying to psyche me out. I was disappointed, but it wasn't going to break me. If I was lucky, maybe they'd let Will visit later.

The two prosecution lawyers sat on the other side of the aisle—a greying man with a beard, and his forty-something offsider, both in expensive suits and blue silk ties. The older one turned and met my gaze. His hard stare sent a shiver of fear through me, but I raised my chin and sent a defiant glare his way. A smidge of surprise registered on his face. *Yeah, you're not going to scare me. Okay, so you do scare me, but I'm pretending.* I didn't want to give these thugs the satisfaction of seeing me cowed.

The door opened, and I turned.

My Aussie nemesis. His eyes found me straight away, and there was that smarmy look on his face. It was lucky I had magic-blocking cuffs on right now, or I wouldn't have been able to contain myself.

I turned back to the front of the room. An older woman stood at another door, hands folded in front of herself. "All rise for Judge Templeton." We stood.

Judge Templeton strode through the door. A fifty-something-year-old woman wearing a short judge's wig, stylish purple-framed glasses, and black robes, she gave off an air of supreme confidence, and like Angelica, she looked like she didn't suffer fools. I hoped this was my lucky day.

The judge sat. She eyed the prosecution lawyers, then me. Her poker face was sterner than Angelica's, if that were even possible, and she gave nothing away. Maybe my earlier assessment wasn't going to work in my favour. She didn't look like the warmest of people. She opened the black folder on her table, then pinned me with her gaze. "Please stand, Miss Lily Bianchi." I did as asked, my heart thudding so hard it vibrated in my ears. I breathed deeply, trying to douse the adrenaline flooding my system. She read out the charges, which sounded even worse in this overly formal environment. "These are some serious charges, Miss Bianchi. How do you plead?"

When my voice came out, I was surprised it wasn't shaky. "Not guilty, Your Honour." Well, I was sort of guilty, but there was a story with it.

"We have video footage of the event, and it appears as though you did use magic against a non-witch."

Well, that was a punch to the guts. My lawyer had obviously handed them the video. Maybe she thought it was good evidence in my favour. I glanced at Robyn, and she gave a small nod, her expression giving nothing away. When she'd visited me with Angelica and Will, the first thing she told me was to tell the truth, so that's what I was going to do.

"Yes, Your Honour, I did, but—"

She held up her hand and turned to the prosecution. This wasn't going well. *Squirrels, think of the squirrels holding peanuts, nibbling cutely.* "It says here that Miss Bianchi was caught in the act. Is that correct?"

The younger lawyer stood. "Yes, Your Honour. She was caught red-handed by two of ACFCALDOTSPB's best agents." Best agents my behind.

The judge nodded. "And what were the circumstances in which the magic was used?"

The younger lawyer glanced at the older one and sat. The older one stood. "They were in the national park at night."

Judge Templeton's stare intensified. "Don't hold back on any details, counsellor. What was happening in the national park that night?" Hmm, was she doing me a favour?

He cleared his throat, obviously not eager to continue. "Miss Bianchi was there with three of her friends and two others." Templeton gave him a look as if to say "don't push my patience." "It appears as if they were there to… stop…" His voice had lowered so much that the judge had to lean forward to hear him. "A murder."

The judge nodded. "And now we get to the crux of the matter." She sent her stern gaze barrelling down the room. I turned and smiled. Bothers took her attention right in the chest. Ha! "Please come down here, Agent Brothers, and stand with the prosecution. I'd like to ask you some questions."

I looked at Robyn, and her smile was positively evil, but in a good way. She gave me a nod. I had no experience in these types of proceedings, but I was willing to bet a year's supply of double-choc-chip muffins that this was highly irregular.

Bothers traipsed down the aisle, looking for all the world as if he thought he was about to get his promotion on the spot. He gave me a gloating look as he passed. *Argh, get lost.* One half of my upper lip lifted in a sneer. *Oops.* I didn't want to show him that he got to me, but at least it was better than looking scared.

He stood next to the younger lawyer and looked at the judge. The judge stared at him until the silence became uncomfortable. "I understand that you've been tailing Miss Bianchi since she arrived in Sydney. Is that correct?" The question seemed benign.

"Yes, Your Honour. I considered her a possible threat, and I wanted to make sure nothing happened to the good citizens of Sydney."

"Commendable behaviour… if she did actually pose a threat."

Bothers had looked proud of himself until the judge had finished the sentence. He stood straighter, his chin lifting in defiance. "She is a danger, clearly. Look at what she did to that poor woman. She hit her with lightning and cast a freeze spell. It was just lucky I was there to stop her."

The judge looked down at the papers in front of her and leafed through, read something, and looked up. "That *poor woman* you speak of is accused of organising her own sister's murder and is currently awaiting trial because there's enough evidence to warrant it. Surely you're aware of this? I would think an outstanding agent such as yourself would be cognisant of all the facts." My heart soared, and I couldn't hide my smile. Thank the universe this hadn't all been for nothing. Cory was safe, and Frances was going to get justice. The judge glanced at me, then back at Bothers. She probably thought I was smiling at his dressing down. But I hadn't counted my chickens yet.

Bothers' Adam's apple bobbed with his swallow. Ha, I hoped he was squirming. "I, uh...." He took a moment, maybe reminding himself that lying in court was a crime. "Yes, Your Honour, but it doesn—"

"And did you know that Miss Bianchi has provided exemplary service in England in law enforcement and isn't on any watch lists here? It seems as though you have targeted her based on your own misguided observations. Is that correct?"

He swallowed again and brought his hands in front of himself, linking them. "Yes, Your Honour."

"The facts of the matter, as I understand them, show that Miss Bianchi is indeed guilty of using magic; however, she only cast those spells to diffuse a dangerous situation, thereby saving a man's life and solving a murder. Her magic use wasn't reckless and wasn't unreasonable under the circumstances. Your behaviour was, however. I'm recommending that the ACFCALDOTSPB review your appointment immediately."

He paled. Not the outcome he was looking for. Again, this

was probably highly unusual, but I was here for it. I curtailed my grin and kept all the joy on the inside. The judge might not like a gloater.

She turned to me. "Miss Bianchi, I would like to apologise for your treatment since you arrived back home. Your work abroad is clearly exemplary, and you do us proud. My findings are that you acted in an appropriate manner for the situation. Mr Bannister is very lucky you were there that night. I, for one, am glad that two murder suspects are off the streets because of your work. Thank you for going above and beyond while you're supposed to be enjoying a holiday." Wow, she had the lowdown on everything. She looked at the prosecution. "My findings are that Miss Bianchi has no case to answer, and you'll be lucky if she doesn't sue the ACFCALDOTSPB." I did smile outwardly at that. She was probably giving me a hint about what she'd like to see happen, but I didn't have the time or energy for that. Hopefully Bothers would be fired today. That would be restitution enough.

The judge hit Bothers and the prosecution with one final flinty stare and looked at me. "Case dismissed."

Brothers turned to me, fury contorting his face. It was my turn to give him a smug look.

Robyn interrupted my fun times. She stood and gave me a hug. I felt like jumping up and down and cheering, but I threw a thank-you smile the judge's way instead. She returned it.

My wedding was in two days, and I was going to be there for it. Woo-hoo!

Take that, Bothers.

CHAPTER 16

The next day, I stood in line with Michelle, Simone, and Will at Frances's wake. The funeral had been sad and draining, and now it was time to speak to Cory. Hundreds had turned out to say goodbye. She was such a well-liked person in the community. Her distraught mum, wearing black, was being pushed in a wheelchair by a twenty-something woman who'd been introduced as Frances's cousin Mary.

It was finally our turn to give Cory our condolences. His eyes were red and his skin pale. He must've still been in shock to learn about Amy. He'd been living with her after welcoming her into his home. Devastated probably didn't come close to how he felt.

"I'm so sorry about everything, Cory. I wish there was something I could say to make it better." A tear squeezed out of the corner of my eye. Argh, I didn't want to cry and make him feel worse.

He did something unexpected—he pulled me in for a tight

hug. He released me. "Lily, I can't thank you enough for what you've done. Frances was so excited about catering your wedding, and she couldn't stop saying how nice you were. Her praise was gushing, but it didn't begin to cover it. If she knew what you'd done for her... for me, she would've been forever grateful, as I am. A thousand times, thank you. If there's anything I can do for you ever, just call. My door's always open, and you'll have a lifetime of free cappuccinos from Surfer's Brew."

I smiled. "Thank you, Cory. Lucky I'm leaving for England soon, or I'd probably send you broke." I blinked as an unexpected onslaught of tears threatened. "Frances was a beautiful person, and I'll never forget her." Damn, the tears broke through. "If you ever want to just talk about her, give me a call. I have a few stories to share." She'd made me the life-saving coffee the morning Angelica had shown up at my door to tell me I was a witch and that James was missing. Not that I'd tell him I was a witch, but I had a few stories of nights out and fun had. The good times were what we needed to remember.

"I'll be sure to do that, Lily. Thank you, on behalf of me and Frances." A tear slid down his cheek. I gave him another hug.

"Hang in there." I stepped back so that Simone and Michelle could pass on their condolences. Will pulled me to the side and rubbed my back. "You did good, Lily."

"Thanks, but it doesn't make anything better." All the good in the world couldn't bring Frances back.

"I know. I'm sorry."

I gave him a hug. There was nothing to say. I guessed I'd let my tears do the talking today, and boy did they have a lot to say.

Will's parents had flown in last night, so his mum joined us on my hen's night. It had started out a bit sombre because the funeral had been this morning, and Simone and Michelle had still decided to join me. I was happy they had. Good friends were hard to come by, and I'd known them longer than anyone else, well, other than Mum and James.

Everyone had a cocktail in hand, and I'd just finished updating them on everything that had happened, although, as far as Simone and Michelle knew, Bothers had mistakenly thought I was a drug dealer, and that's why I'd been arrested. If only I could tell them about witches. In any case, there hadn't been much time to talk to my English crew since I got home last night with Will's parents flying in and the funeral the next day, plus I'd been exhausted. It had been all I could do to stay awake until 9:00 p.m. Once everything had been explained, I could relax and think about the fun stuff—my wedding.

We didn't spend a lot of time with Will's parents back in England because of work and being in hiding, so I didn't know them well, but Cassandra Blakesley was always nice to me. Tonight she'd been positively brimming with compliments. I wasn't complaining. "I'm so glad Will finally wised up and asked you to marry him. You two are a good match. And Sarah seems to love you too."

I smiled. "I love both of them. They're amazing humans. You and your husband did a good job."

"Thank you, Lily." She looked at Mum. "Kat did a wonderful job too."

Mum smiled. "Thank you, Cassandra."

"Call me Cass."

"Okay, Cass." Mum held up her glass and got our group's attention over the music. "Hey, let's have a toast. To my amazing daughter, Lily, and her equally amazing fiancé, Will." Not that Will was here to hear it. He was out with the boys and his dad. Mum's eyes brimmed with moisture as she looked at me with love. "May you both have a long, happy life together filled with joy, health, and babies."

If Cassandra had knocked her glass against Mum's any harder, they would've broken. Argh, looked like they weren't going to waste time asking when children were coming.

Before I could complain about the babies bit, everyone said, "Cheers!" and clinked glasses. *Oh well, go with the flow.* Besides, how could I really complain? I wasn't in jail—I was here with the people I loved, and yes, Bothers had been fired. I'd make a toast to that later.

Imani threw her arm around me. "It's so good to have you back, love. We missed you."

Liv piled in, some of her drink sloshing out of her glass. "I cried when I heard you were in jail. I can't imagine how you felt."

"It's certainly good to be free… again." I looked at Imani. "Thank you for helping get to the bottom of everything too. Frances would thank you if she knew."

"All in a day's work." She winked. "Now, it looks like your drink is running low. I might just have to go to the bar."

Before I could say no—I was trying in vain to pace myself, but everyone kept getting me another drink—"Nutbush City Limits" by Tina Turner came on. Michelle and Simone screamed and each grabbed one of my arms. Women around the room ran for the dance floor. It was like a tide of hungry squirrels scrambling for the nut bowl. "Oh my God. We have to dance to this!" Michelle shouted. She started for the dance floor, dragging me and Simone with her. I managed to plonk my drink down on a random table. Sarah, Millicent, and Liv laughed and followed us.

Everyone had formed lines on the dance floor, and as Tina belted the words out in her gravelly voice, we partook in a ritual as old as time… well as old as at least the 80s. I found my place in the crowd and stepped my right foot out to the side twice, then my left. Then my right foot kicked out to the back twice, then the left foot. After that, it was right elbow to right knee twice, and then the left. I was totally working up a sweat amongst the frenzied dancers. Then we did some weird thing with our feet and turned 90 degrees to the left and started again.

Sarah, Millicent, and Liv were laughing and trying to copy everything. They managed to perfect it on the third direction change. The hypnotic beat had everyone enthusiastically busting out the moves in sync. "This is wild," Sarah yelled.

I laughed. "I know. Only in Australia." I looked at Michelle and Simone—they were grinning and having an awesome time. Maybe this was just what we all needed after saying goodbye to Frances.

When the song finished, we took our puffed-out selves back to Mum, Imani, and Cass. Imani handed me a new drink. If I wasn't careful, I was going to have the mother of all hangovers tomorrow. Michelle and Simone grabbed their drinks off the table—Mum had been keeping an eye on them because drink spiking was always a risk.

I held my glass up and raised my voice to be heard over the music. "Ladies, I want to say thank you so much for cele-brating with me tonight." I looked at each of them in turn. "You all mean the world to me." They smiled. I swallowed against a rush of emotion and looked at Simone and Michelle.

"Let's drink to the fact that we were able to know the amazing woman that was Frances—may she be watching us and celebrating with us, and may we never forget her." My two friends chinked their glasses against mine, and we had a quick sip. I raised my glass again. "My next and last toast is for all of you. Thank you for sticking with me and my craziness, and may we all get many more years together. I love you, ladies. Cheers!" As I drained my cocktail, I soaked up the joy of the moment.

As we lowered our glasses, "Love Shack" came on. Sarah's eyes lit up. She grabbed my arm. "Time for another dance. It's party time, squirrel girl. We're gonna shut this place down!" As she led me to the dance floor and everyone followed, I had no doubt we were.

CHAPTER 17

The night before the wedding, Will and the boys stayed at a hotel in the city. I didn't subscribe to the bad-luck-to-see-each-other-before-the-wedding thing, but it was convenient. All us ladies needed space to get ready. With two hairstylists and two make-up artists working on us, it was a frantic scene. Mum had hired a caterer for the wedding—we were fortunate they'd had a last-minute cancellation. How I got so lucky, who knew, but I wasn't going to argue. They'd sent two staff here to serve us champagne and hors d'oeuvres so we wouldn't be starving by this afternoon. It was all very civilised.

And now it was time to dress. I couldn't quite believe the moment had come. It had taken incredible sacrifice and determination to get here. But it had all been worth it. I'd learned so much about myself, found my mum, and formed some of the closest friendships I'd ever had. What had seemed like a tragic event—James being kidnapped—had turned into one of the pivotal moments of my life.

It had led to Will.

Now here I stood in my old room. My life had come full circle. I stared at the dress laid out on the bed and smiled. I was getting married today.

Someone knocked on the door. I turned. "Come in."

Mum opened the door and came in. "How's my gorgeous girl?" She gave me a hug.

"I'm good, thanks." I leaned away so I could look in her eyes. "Thanks for everything. You've gone above and beyond. So far, it's been the best day ever."

She beamed. "It's not nearly over yet. I brought something for you. Angelica found out from James where he'd stored a lot of family things he wasn't ready to part with. In it was this." She handed me a blue handkerchief with my father's initials embroidered on it. "Something old and something blue." Sadness crept into her voice. "Your father had this in his pocket on our wedding day. I'd like you to slip it around the flower stalks, and after you say your vows, you can give it to Will. Your dad would be so proud of you today, sweetie. You've turned into an extraordinary woman. I'm just so sorry he's not here to share your special day and walk you down the aisle." Her voice shook at the end.

My face scrunched up as I fought not to cry. "Thank you." I wanted to say I wished he were here, but acknowledging that would make me sob, so I said nothing. Instead, I lifted the handkerchief to my nose and breathed in. Though old, it held a note of the scent of dad's aftershave. A hundred memories flooded back to me. *I miss you, Dad.*

Mum slid her arms around my waist and squeezed tight. "Try not to cry. The make-up ladies are leaving soon."

I chuckled through slowly leaking tears. "Okay. I think I'll need a touch-up before they go."

"I'll tell them not to leave just yet. Put your dress on, and no more crying. Okay?"

I nodded. "Okay."

The door was open, but another knock came. We turned. Imani, Liv, Millicent, Angelica, Cassandra, and Sarah stood there. My ladies. My family. "Can we come in?" Sarah asked.

I smiled. "Of course."

Liv stood in front of me. "We know your mum gave you the handkerchief, so I've got the something borrowed." She handed me a delicate gold ankle bracelet. "My parents gave me that for my twenty-first birthday, and it's brought me good luck. Every time I wear it, lovely things happen. I'd love for you to wear it today."

"Thank you! I would love to wear this." I hugged her.

Imani stared at me, her face suddenly serious. She held a black velvet box in her hand. "We all put in and got you this, love." She bit her bottom lip and paused, maybe fighting her emotions. She normally didn't get teary, but I could see the telltale glistening in her eyes. She handed it to me.

I ran my fingertips over the soft surface. "You shouldn't have."

Angelica smiled. "Come on, dear. Open it. You don't want to be late for your wedding."

I slowly lifted the lid. A bracelet, a string of small golden hearts joined together, lay on the dark velvet interior. I took it out and examined it. On the backs of some of the hearts were small engravings. "This has all your names." I looked at each woman in turn. "This is amazing. You ladies are the best. I love it!" I handed the box to Imani and asked Liv to help put it on. It would end up under my white gloves, but that was okay. I'd probably rarely take it off. This symbolised the love of friends who had become family. "I feel like the luckiest person in the world today. Thank you all for standing by me, and for coming all this way for Will and me. You all blow me away."

"We're the lucky ones," Sarah said. "You took the annoying William off our hands." She looked at her mum, and they both laughed.

"And one day, you'll give Annabelle a cousin." Millicent smirked.

"Give us five minutes of fun before you wish that on us." I laughed.

Angelica looked at me. "The day you opened that door to me is one I will never forget. I know I was hard on you, but I saw your potential from the get-go, not to mention how much like your mother you looked. You've been a joy to have around, Lily, and I honestly don't know where the PIB would be without you, or where I would be. I will always be here for you." She looked at Mum, and they both smiled.

This was so out of character, I wasn't sure what to say. "Um, wow. I'm used to you berating me. I know it hasn't been easy, but I do appreciate that you push me to be my best. And thanks for helping me get my mum back." The fact that Mum was here today was a miracle, and I would appreciate every minute of it.

Imani spoke up. "Okay, I think it's time to let Lily dress, or we'll be late."

Everyone piled out and left me and Mum to it, as I needed her to do up the small buttons on the back of the dress. When I was ready, the make-up lady fixed my tear tracks, and then we were ready to go.

Two classic white Jaguars waited outside to drive us the hour and quarter to Mosman. This was really happening. *Eek!* My stomach did a couple of little flips as I got in. Maybe I shouldn't have had that second champagne, or maybe it was the double-chocolate-chip muffin. Apparently Will had made Mum promise to get it for me. He was so sweet. It was probably lucky I fitted into my dress after all that.

I fidgeted so much on the way that Imani took my bouquet off me. I didn't know why I was nervous. Will was the man I wanted to spend the rest of my life with, and this was the day I'd held on for through every harrowing day fighting the directors. I took a few deep breaths as we pulled up to the sandstone and iron gates. Mum's friend was, apparently, mega-loaded. A waterfront in one of Sydney's most exclusive suburbs didn't come cheap.

The gates opened, and in we drove, past immaculately trimmed green hedges and a fountain. Impressive.

James was at the huge timber front door of the three-storey turn-of-the-century home. He and Mum were walking me down the aisle. Liv was my bridesmaid, and Beren was the best man. Millicent was carrying Annabelle down the aisle while she gave her rose petals to throw. This was going to be adorable.

As soon as James saw me, his face softened. "You look beautiful."

"Thank you. You look rather spiffy yourself." My brother scrubbed up well. Millicent gave him an appreciative stare.

He grinned at her. "And look at you, my gorgeous lady." He kissed her. Mum looked on, a dreamy expression on her face. She was in her element. Her kids were happy, and she was here to see it. My heart filled with joy.

Imani, ever the sensible one, tapped her wrist. "It's time. Don't leave poor Will waiting. He might decide to leave." She snorted.

"More cake for me." I stuck my tongue out at her.

"Oh God, how much cake are you going to eat?" she asked. "Didn't you end up getting the three-tiered one?"

"Um, yes. I meant to get the two-tiered one, but I wanted three flavours—chocolate, coconut, and lemon."

"Of course you did." She shook her head and looked at my wedding dress. "At least you only have to fit into this for one day."

Sarah laughed. "So cruel. Come on. Let's get a move on. My poor brother is probably ready to come out and grab her." She led her mother and almost everyone else inside. I stood at the front door with Mum and James, Millicent at the front holding Annabelle, and Liv behind them.

The music started.

I gripped my bouquet and willed my nerves to settle.

What if I tripped? Argh, stop it. You're not going to trip.

I touched the heart bracelet on my wrist and thought about the love that was with me today. It was going to be okay. Even if I tripped and fell, there were people here who would pick me up and dust me off, make sure I was okay.

A red carpet had been laid out through the hallway that ran half the length of the house. The carpet continued into a vaulted-ceilinged kitchen/living room. Huge, blue-glazed pots lined either side of the carpet, white roses bursting from each one. The scent was divine. Once we reached the open back french doors, Millicent gave Annabelle the go-ahead to grab the white petals and throw. She giggled as her chubby little hands dove into the box.

The vast back patio was limestone tiled and covered by a timber pergola. Grape vines covered the structure, the after-noon sunlight peeking through the leaves. As I peered out onto the level lawn, the blue of the magnificent harbour glinted back at me. But that was nothing compared to the man who stood between me and the water.

Our eyes locked, and my stomach somersaulted. He still did that to me. Which was probably a good thing since we were getting married. His grey-blue eyes reflected the peacock-blue of his vest, his sexy gaze more beautiful than ever. He was a sight to behold. How was this my man?

We reached the end of the carpet, and James and Mum kissed my cheeks. James shook Will's hand, and Mum gave him a heartfelt hug, then she took my hand and placed it in his. She gave me a last kiss on the cheek and took her seat next to James in the front row. Beren gave me an encouraging look, then grinned at Liv.

What everyone else did next, I had no idea because all I could do was stare at my soon-to-be husband. He squeezed my hands. "You look incredible. The most stunning woman I've ever seen. I love you."

The celebrant cleared her throat. "Let's stick to the vows for now." She smiled and got started. We'd agreed that we wanted something simple that wouldn't go on forever, so we didn't have anything but the celebrant and then our vows.

"Do you, Lily Bianchi, take William Blakesley to be your lawfully wedded husband, to love whether there are double-chocolate-chip muffins or not, to be patient with him even when he becomes Agent Crankypants, and do you agree to always help him find his phone or keys when he loses them, no matter if it's the third time that week, for as long as you both shall live?"

A snort rang out, which was probably Imani. Will was trying not to laugh—I hadn't okayed my part of the vows with him beforehand. I grinned. "I do." I slipped the ring on his finger.

"And do you, William Blakesley, take Lily Bianchi to be your lawfully wedded wife, in the good times and the bad, even when she's a crazy old squirrel lady? Do you promise to laugh at her bad jokes and not laugh when she's unintentionally done something silly? Do you promise to keep her in double-chocolate-chip muffins and cappuccinos for as long as you both shall live?"

I chuckled. He grinned, his dimples coming out to play. "I do." He placed the gold ring on my finger and kissed my hand. He was such a keeper.

I now pronounce you husband and wife. "You may kiss each other."

As he stared down at me, joy warmed my insides, expanding until I felt I would burst. He put his arms around me and leaned down. His soft lips met mine. Our first kiss as husband and wife. It was the best kiss in the universe. Even better, there'd be many more to come.

When everyone started whooping, we pulled apart. Hmm, we didn't want to give them too much of a show, and I had to admit that it was easy to get carried away while kissing Will.

We turned and looked at our grinning friends and family, who were all on their feet, coming towards us. They swept us up in the group hug of the century, engulfing us with love. Everything we'd all been through to get here had been worth it. Every missed minute of freedom, every painful, scary, heartbreaking moment. And I'd do it all again for anyone here.

But that was a thought for another day.

Right now, it was time to enjoy the best day of my life, so I pulled Will to me and kissed him again.

When we were done, he waggled his brows. "I know what you want."

I blushed. "And what would that be?"

"Cake." He grinned.

I laughed. "You're a keeper, Mr Blakesley."

"As long as you're doing the keeping, I'm in, Mrs Blakesley. Welcome to the rest of our lives."

James handed us each a champagne, and everyone gathered around, drinks in hand. "What are we drinking to, to start?" My brother winked. Yes, there would be many toasts today.

I smiled. "To the love of friends and family, and to the best future ever!"

A chorus of "Cheers!" rang out. Whatever had been and whatever may come, I would cherish today for the rest of my life. And just when I thought it couldn't get any better, Sarah started clinking her wine glass with a spoon. Others followed until the tinkling reached fever pitch.

Love shone from Will's eyes as he gazed down at me. "Hey, Mrs Blakesley, I think they want us to kiss."

I grinned. "Well, Mr Blakesley, what are you waiting for?"

Book 21 in the PIB series will be out 31st July, 2023.

In the meantime, if you'd like to try my ghost cosy mystery series—Haunting Avery Winters—you can order book 1, A Killer Welcome, online or from your local bookstore.

Avery Winters was overjoyed to be brought back to life... unfortunately, the dead were waiting for her.

Aussie journalist Avery Winters was content—she had a caring boyfriend, great job, and supportive… okay, so her parents weren't actually supportive, but she'd accepted she could never be the son they'd wanted seeing as how she was born a girl. Avoiding them seemed to work well, and, she reasoned, no one's life was perfect. And that was fine, except whilst covering a news story in a storm, Avery's cosy life disappeared in a flash. Lightning struck, stopping her heart and blowing her favourite black boots to smithereens. It was pure luck that an off-duty nurse was walking nearby.

When Avery came to in the ambulance en route to hospital, she'd thought the worst was over. She was wrong. Her lightning-induced hallucinations—there was no way they were ghosts—were impossible to hide. Her boyfriend soon left, and her boss suggested she take extended leave. Unable to cover her rent, she moved back in with her parents. And that's when the fun really began. Unable to cope with their insistence she was crazy, and desperate for an escape, she responded to a journalist-wanted ad… in the UK, because getting mega far away from her parents could only be a good thing.

Armed with a new fear of storms, companions others couldn't see, and the hope that leaving the stress behind would improve her mental state, she boarded a plane for London. What she didn't count on was not being able to leave her ghosts behind… literally.

Oh, and that the quaint English village she'd be living in had more skeletons in its closet than the Natural History Museum. When she stumbles upon a dead body in her rented apartment on her first day, she's tempted to get back on the plane. But whilst it's not a good omen, returning to her parents would be worse, so she decides to stay.

Only, she's not sure if it's the best decision she's ever made, or the worst. She's about to find out.

ALSO BY DIONNE LISTER

Paranormal Investigation Bureau

Witchnapped in Westerham #1

Witch Swindled in Westerham #2

Witch Undercover in Westerham #3

Witchslapped in Westerham #4

Witch Silenced in Westerham #5

Killer Witch in Westerham #6

Witch Haunted in Westerham #7

Witch Oracle in Westerham #8

Witchbotched in Westerham #9

Witch Cursed in Westerham #10

Witch Heist in Westerham #11

Witch Burglar in Westerham #12

Vampire Witch in Westerham #13

Witch War in Westerham #14

Westerham Witches and a Venetian Vendetta #15

Witch Nemesis in Westerham #16

Witch Catastrophe in Westerham #17

Witch Karma in Westerham Book #18

Witch Showdown in Westerham Book #19

Westerham Witches and an Aussie Misadventure Book #20

Book #21 (coming July 2023)

Christmissing in Westerham (Christmas novella)

Haunting Avery Winters

(Paranormal Cosy Mystery)

A Killer Welcome #1

A Regrettable Roast #2

A Fallow Grave #3

A Frozen Stiff #4

A Deadly Drive-by #5

A Caffeine Fix #6 (Coming May 2023)

The Circle of Talia

(YA Epic Fantasy)

Shadows of the Realm

A Time of Darkness

Realm of Blood and Fire

The Rose of Nerine

(Epic Fantasy)

Tempering the Rose

Forging the Rose

ABOUT THE AUTHOR

USA Today bestselling author, Dionne Lister is a Sydneysider with a degree in creative writing and two Siamese cats. Daydreaming has always been her passion, so writing was a natural progression from staring out the window in primary school, and being an author was a dream she held since childhood.

Unfortunately, writing was only a hobby while Dionne worked as a property valuer in Sydney, until her mid-thirties when she returned to study and completed her creative writing degree. Since then, she has indulged her passion for writing while raising two children with her husband. Her books have attracted praise from Apple iBooks and have reached #1 on Amazon and iBooks charts worldwide, frequently occupying top 100 lists in fantasy and mystery.

Printed in Great Britain
by Amazon